AF255133

# Outpatient

A Story of Horror
and Madness

# OutPatient

By Clifford Beck

*For My Brother, Randy.*

"Wherever you go,
There you are."

Anonymous

Chapter 1


The cabin stood at the end of Stratton Brooke Road, a few yards away from the pond, surrounded by the isolated woods of Carrabasset Valley, overlooking the southern face of Mount Bigelow, standing as a monument to time and nature. Autumn brought a palette of colors that burned across the mountain and dipped down into the valley, while winter laid out a chilly blanket of white, leaving only the rock of the southern face to bear itself out. In the snow, she could easily follow the multitude of tiny mouse tracks that barely left their mark in the fine crystalline covering of old man winter's silver blue. It was August and the heat was at its peak, with small bursts of rain moving through almost daily like curtains of gray crawling across the sky. The valley seemed to be a magnet for turbulent weather this year, but so far, there were no real problems – it was just rain.

A glimpse of its exterior cast a well-ordered reflection of who would live inside. But this façade, in time, would only prove to be an illusion – well-built walls of protection for the chaos that now takes sanctuary within. There is a tense quiet in the house, as though its occupants were merely ghosts quietly sleeping among the attic rafters.

And all around, in every room, lay scattered the articles of a previous existence. But that was when life held out a promise of the future.  A singular photograph, framed in pewter, was the only image that graced the mantle – a strikingly beautiful woman at the peak of her youth, dressed in the academic garb of graduation. To her left, a middle-aged man in a simple business suit, a hand on her shoulder and the proud smile of a father's love stretched across his face. Written on the upper left were neatly penned the words, 'Congratulations, Cat. Love, Dad!' This single portrait lay surrounded by all things feline. Even the clock on the wall that ticked and tocked, marking the inevitable march of time, slowly scanned the room with its black and white eyes at every sweep of its plastic tail. Not far from the mantle, another frame clung to the wall, larger than the first. A beautiful document lay inside the frame – 'Bowdoin College, department of Physics, Physician's Degree, Catherine Thomaston'. The signatures of the President and department chair were scrawled across the bottom left.

The kitchen was spotless and presented itself with the odor of numerous cleaning products. But upon closer examination, something was amiss. There was not one knife to be seen – not on any counter; not in any drawer. In fact, there were no knives in this kitchen – perhaps in the entire house. Toward the back, a bedroom door stood slightly ajar, and on the bed of this spartan room lay a woman in her thirties. Her auburn hair cut short with a pair of sewing scissors – her body now merely a shell of the romanesque figure she once possessed. She began to noticeably perspire as her eyes darted from side to side as if her mind had taken residence in another place and time, where the universe of what was real stood still in its celestial motion. And it was in this chaotic world she heard the tapping sound of steps slowly making their way down a darkened corridor, dimly lit by a pair of lights mounted high upon the wall. With bare feet lightly walking the cold linoleum floor, she cautiously wandered her way through a strangely familiar place. Her name was whispered from the air behind her, and she spun around, startled into a heavy sweat, to find no one. With foreboding hesitation, she turned back again, gasped, and screamed in terror as the hallway lay transformed. Rusty cages lined the walls, bound shut by locks and chains from a bygone era. And from behind those bars reached out to her the filthy hands of the disrobed insane. Rattling their bars and screaming in madness, they seemed to reach out from everywhere, grabbing at her shoulders and pulling at her hair. With arms covering her head, she turned in each direction, looking for escape. And in a sudden scream of panic, the hallway once again lay empty. She held her breath in uncertainty with fingers pressed upon her mouth and tears streaming down her face. Feeling a sharp sting enter deeply into her shoulder, she quickly turned to investigate. She was startled to find an elderly nurse with eyes a hauntingly solid black and a bony thumb pushing down the plunger of a hypodermic needle. She gasped again in disbelief, and her vision slowly blurred to a field of white, then collapsed into the blackness of nonexistence.

She bolted up in bed, hands firmly gripping the sheet around her throat. Her face and hair soaked with sweat, her eyes darting about the room, being certain that she was alone. In a moment of confusion, Catherine glanced over at her shoulder and, finding it unmarked, breathed a sigh of relief as she wiped the sweat from her face. She turned, put her feet on the floor beside the bed, stood, and slowly wove her way down the hall and into the bathroom. She turned a slightly rusted faucet that let out a somewhat piercing squeal, as cold water flowed out into her hands. When it was nearly overflowing, she brought the water to her face and held it to her skin, letting the cold and wet sink deeply, washing away the sweat and steadying her nerves. As she brought her hands away from her face, the cool water slightly warmed by her waking flesh dripped from her eyelashes and ran off her nose and lips. Catherine raised her head and noticed a familiar face staring back from the streaked bathroom mirror.

Momentarily, her gaze froze on the eyes that lay inside the glass; as though they belonged to someone she'd never met. But, her gaze was broken by the sudden realization that water still flowed from the bathroom tap.

Standing in the shower Catherine crossed her arms tightly over her breasts as she stood beneath the spray of warming water running down her naked body. Stepping out onto a plush green mat, she pushed her toes into its soft, deep nap. This was one of the few pleasures Catherine had in her life. The other was coffee – sweet nectar of God incarnate – a divine gift to a weary world. And after she toweled off her hair and body, she walked into the kitchen, her head wrapped in a towel and dressed in a white cotton robe. She preferred her coffee black and steaming hot, bringing her senses back to life after another night of disturbed sleep. She left the kitchen with coffee mug in hand, holding it carefully so as not to lose a single precious drop. And entering her living room, went straight to the framed photo on the mantle where she stood gazing at the face of the man who departed from her life – the only man she thought ever truly loved her. Every morning, she approached the photo, still sick at heart with the pain of grief. She gently stroked a finger down the face of the man in the photo.

"Good morning, daddy", she whispered in an almost childlike voice.

Catherine quietly kissed the tip of her finger and touched it back to the man's face, not noticing her image smiling back from his side. She placed her now half-filled mug on the coffee table that was arranged between the mantle and the couch. The furniture of her small cabin was arranged as though the house had been built around it, unchanging and ordered – almost to a fault. There were opened bills on the coffee table staring up at her – power, cable, phone, water, and mortgage. These would all be dealt with, as her father made certain of that when he left a retirement trust for her in the amount of some seven million dollars. She had been forced to leave her job as a professor of theoretical physics at Bowdoin College and since the onset of her illness; Catherine was no longer able to teach, as her thinking had become disabled by the loss of who she had been.

She looked down at the coffee table again, this time with focused intent. A manila folder sat patiently waiting for her examination. It was a good two inches thick and in bold stenciled letters blazing across the front read, 'Augusta Mental Health Institute'. Catherine had made a special request for a copy of her records in order to satisfy her craving for a deeper understanding of an illness that no one can touch or see, as there was no blood test for schizophrenia.

She skipped over everything else and flipped to the psychiatric note written just before her discharge. But just before giving the document her full attention, she felt something soft push against the top of her ankle. Looking down, a rare smile came to her face as her eyes looked into the caring gaze of her cat. Ivan was her constant companion. A solid smoky gray Russian Blue with striking golden eyes and a gaze that gave him a look of understanding. Catherine relied upon his silent feline wisdom as though he was her father confessor. She leaned back on the couch and Ivan leaped up into her lap. It was always a welcomed place and a great source of comfort for him. Catherine picked him up and laid him on her chest. She spoke to him in baby talk, like anyone else who happened to be owned by a cat. Licking her chin and loudly purring brought a broad smile to her face.

"Mommy loves you too", she whispered into Ivan's ear. "But she has things to do before she goes to see the doctor".

As though he understood, Ivan gently jumped down from Catherine's chest and onto the cushion at the end of the couch, where he curled up in a ball and closed his eyes. And with the end of his tail covering his nose, Ivan began to gently purr as he drifted off to sleep. Catherine could now direct her attention back to the documents that lay on the table in front of her. She poured over them for

about forty-five minutes, reflecting on the course
of her life and the events that led to such a painful
existence.

Chapter 2

She grew up in Farmington after her family left Augusta when her father William was appointed to the position of president at the University of Maine. Catherine was always very close to her father, and he spent many evenings outside looking at the stars. Her father pointed out the constellations to her and after a few months, she had memorized all of them. For Christmas, her father bought her a Celestron 10-inch telescope with a motorized mount and an electronic directional guide. It wasn't soon after this that Catherine picked up a book on astronomy and was studying the skies on every clear night. She was even outside studying Orion's belt in December. Her mother, Emily, had warned Catherine repeatedly about being out in the cold.

"Catherine, you'll catch your death of cold!" she'd say.

"Emily, she'll be fine," William would say.

"She knows what time to come in." Catherine would look at her watch.

"Darn, nine o'clock already?" she'd say to herself.

So, she'd turn everything off and start carrying it into the house. Once she got through the door, her father would glance at her mother with a reassuring nod. And when Catherine disappeared into her room, her mother would remark about how much of a 'daddy's girl' she was.

Her brother, Robert, was already in high school studying for his SATs. He was trying to decide which direction he would go in. He knew he wanted to study psychology, but he wasn't sure if he wanted to go to New York for the Doctor of Psychology program or take the long road through the undergraduate program, then on to graduate school. The Doctor of Psychology program would cut his academic time in half, but the traditional route would give him a broader education. Eventually, he decided to take the long road, acquiring what he believed was a real education. By the time Robert was nearing graduation from his undergraduate program, Catherine was well into high school. Now, her interest in astronomy had begun to blossom, as she has started taking classes in physics and Buddhism.
"Why Buddhism?" her father asked.
She said that deep down she'd always believed that the sciences, on some level, have to merge with spirituality and religion in order to provide a more accurate description of the universe.

Catherine grew up an avid Star Trek fan, and in her youthful imagination, she'd travel daily with the Enterprise crew into the distant universe, visiting strange alien worlds. And after the Hubble Space Telescope released images from the deep view project, she became even more fascinated with the cosmos. She graduated valedictorian from high school and was accepted to the University of Maine at Farmington. And because her father was the president of the college, she would have been able to attend tuition-free. But Catherine had other plans and decided to go to Bowdoin College in Brunswick.

"You know," her father said. "You can get a decent education right here in Farmington."

"I know," Catherine replied. "But Bowdoin has a great physics program and eventually, I can do all my graduate work there. And who knows, I may end up teaching there."

"Any other reasons?" her father inquired.

"Well, they do have a really nice observatory," she responded. "That's not the biggest reason, but it's near the top of the list."

"You and the stars, huh?" he said.

"It's not just the stars," she replied. "It's everything. There's so much more that we just don't understand, and I want to be part of something bigger – something with the real possibility of discovery. Besides, it's your fault – all those nights teaching me the constellations." Catherine affectionately nudged him, and he reacted with a smile.

"Alright, you got me," he said.

"Do I get to tell mom that I'm going?" she asked.

"Sure," her father answered. "Just don't tell her you backed me into a corner about it."

"She's going to know anyway," she teased.

"Yeah, I know," he said. "Your mom's always been like that, hasn't she?"

It wasn't soon after, that Catherine had packed up her car and started the drive to Bowdoin. Her parents decided to follow along, because they wanted to see her off to college, and they were curious about what the campus looked like. After they said their goodbyes, Catherine started toward her assigned dormitory but momentarily glanced back at her father, who seemed to feel her eyes on him. He looked up at her while she blew him a kiss goodbye. She'd only be gone a semester and would then return home for break. Catherine immediately dove into her studies, taking classes in physics, astronomy, comparative religion, and, of course, philosophy. She wanted to gain as broad an understanding as possible of the workings of what she referred to as 'the inner universe' and 'the universe at large'.

# Chapter 3


She rose from the couch with the document still in hand and, making her way into the kitchen, opened the refrigerator door.

"Shit!" she muttered to herself. She'd have to order groceries.

Catherine didn't like going into town. People made her nervous and she felt as though their eyes were constantly upon her, criticizing her every thought. She made her breakfast from what little there was – two eggs, scrambled; two slices of toast, no butter – and of course, coffee. She continued pouring over her psychiatric history, along with the notes written about her treatment at AMHI. Catherine could easily write a thesis on the confluence of energy into matter during the creation of the universe, but 'psycho-speak' was not something she was ordinarily familiar with – thank God there was the Internet. She slid the documents back on the coffee table next to the folder marked 'AMHI' and retreated into her bedroom, with Ivan close behind.


It seemed he was wherever Catherine was, always watching over her. Catherine quickly emerged back into the living room, dressed in cut-off shorts and a gray tank top. She turned on a small radio and tuned it into her favorite a.m. talk show. She needed the stimulation but refused to buy a television. She saw the problems of a world gone mad and took them a bit too close to heart. War, poverty, starvation, genocide – whatever it was driving humanity over the edge toward extinction. Then, after a series of blaring tones, she heard a weather report. There was a large storm headed in her direction, moving northeast from southern New Hampshire. It was a previously recorded announcement, so there were no details on the size or destructive force of the storm. But, it was still in southern New Hampshire, and Catherine browsed the web for almost an hour – there had to be something good happening out there. 'World rejoices as miners in Chile are rescued'.

"Finally", she whispered to herself. A little good news always lifted her spirits, knowing that the world was not an entirely evil place. She read a few more articles while Ivan drifted off on her lap. His whiskers and paws twitched as he lay dreaming about whatever it is that cats dream about. Before she logged off, Catherine ordered her groceries. It was always the same list of items every week, and she kept it on the grocery store's website. She could change it whenever she wanted and order with the click of a mouse. It was an incredible time saver and spared her the discomfort of being around people.

After shutting down her laptop, she got up, still sipping from her coffee, and wandered over

to where her diploma hung on the wall. She gazed
at it deeply and was gently overtaken by
memories of those wonderful days. As a teacher,
her favorite subject was relativity with its
expenses of complex equations, like a beautiful
language that few people truly understood. She
especially enjoyed discussing the anthropocentric
illusion of time, as well as the thought
experiments of Einstein. But for Catherine, it was
more than numbers and symbols. It was an art that
transcended all things and was an expression of
the fundamentals of creation itself.

She took a sudden breath and found herself
back in her house – having left the memories of
better days behind. Then, from out of nowhere, a
wisp of smoke filled her nose. Her mind flew into
a panic with a million racing thoughts. She ran
frantically around her house, checking the stove
and peering up the chimney. She slid her hands
across the walls, looking for warm spots near the
wiring, and ran up into the attic, then down into
the cellar. The thought of a fire only caused the
smell to become more intense. But when she
paused in an attempt to regain her senses, she
realized that the air was free of smoke.

"Fuck!" she yelled, grabbing her hair with
both hands and falling to her knees, weeping in
fear of her sanity. Catherine had no idea what
brought this on. She may have just missed a dose
of her medication. Yes, that must be it. She got to

her feet, still crying, and stumbled out her front door, she sat down on the stoop and lit a cigarette, staring at it in disbelief as she held it between her fingers. She knew it made no sense at all – being a smoker and having the occasional hallucination of smelling smoke. But it did calm her nerves, as she couldn't take a sedative and expect to drive to her appointment at Franklin Memorial.

She knew what smoking could do to her. She saw the consequences of it on the internet once in a while. She imagined her couch catching fire from a lit cigarette, dangling between her fingers as she dozed off into a deep sleep – the house burning around her. Later, after the fire had been extinguished, her body would be found – a shrunken mass of twisted bone and fluid, contained within an unrecognizable charred husk. Catherine would quit this filthy habit someday, but today would not be that day. She only smoked half of it, dropping the rest to the ground and crushing it beneath her shoe. Catherine noticed that her hands were still trembling, but she was still able to get back on her feet. She went back into the house and checked her medication schedule. The antipsychotics she took affected her short-term memory, so she had to mark every dose as she took it. That morning's checkbox was blank, so she took them according to the directions on the label and penned in a check mark on the schedule. On one occasion, she took her morning meds and forgot to mark it on the schedule. She ended up taking a double dose and when she started to become confused, she called an ambulance. She was taken to Franklin Memorial Hospital, then, later, flown by life flight to Maine Medical Center in Portland. Franklin Memorial could have dealt with Catherine's condition, but she had a complicated history and was on some very powerful drugs. She was admitted to the kidney unit on the fifth floor of the Richards wing in order to have her blood cleansed by dialysis. The Narcan they gave her at Franklin Memorial counteracted the effects of the Thiothixene and Clozapine. But the doctors wanted to avoid any acute kidney damage, and they decided to insert a Tesio line directly into her bloodstream near her collarbone. After they spoke with Catherine's psychiatrist, the event was determined to be accidental. So the placement of the Tesio line would be very temporary and would be removed shortly before her discharge.

She had a calendar for everything – all her medical appointments, her menstrual cycle when bills were due, and birthdays – including her father's but excluding her own. Even Ivan's birthday was on the calendar, and Catherine celebrated his birthday with more excitement than anything else. Loyalty wasn't exactly typical in cats, but Ivan was special. He seemed to be not just her companion, but her guardian – following her around the house like a puppy.

Catherine decided that what she needed now was to get out of the house. Stratton Pond was right outside her front door, and she went there often. She especially enjoyed the walk around the pond during the peak of autumn, when Bigelow Mountain's foliage was ablaze with color. The multitude of colors spread out across the majestic mountain range. This helped Catherine to gain some perspective and made the problems of her life seem just a bit smaller. It was just small enough to hike in about an hour or so and as long as she stayed within sight of the water, she wouldn't have to worry about wandering from the pond and getting lost. On one weekend, Catherine decided to hike the trail to Little Bigelow Mountain. She wasn't exactly in shape, but she'd always wanted to try a hike that looked fairly easy and still find a place with a great view. But she didn't know how to prepare for even a small summit hike, and by the time Catherine got to the peak of Little Bigelow she had become badly dehydrated. When her mother was unable to reach her, she called the state police as well as the Bigelow Park service and e-mailed Catherine's picture to them. She was later found trying to make her way down the mountain, covered with cuts and bruises from tripping over her own feet. Catherine spent a night in Franklin Memorial for rehydration therapy and in spite of what she would later think of as a near-death experience, she wanted to get back into the mountains. But the next time, she wanted to be prepared and hindsight being twenty-twenty, she later decided that making her first hike into Mt. Bigelow in the middle of July was probably a bad idea from the start. So, a couple of weeks after her recovery, Catherine picked up the phone and called Nancy.

# Chapter 4

They met as freshmen at Bowdoin College shortly after Catherine moved on campus. She found that living in a college dormitory was anything but peaceful, and eventually, she'd have to move off campus. Renting a small two-bedroom apartment away from the downtown area, she started interviewing potential roommates, offering the second bedroom to someone named Nancy. She was a quiet but spirited young woman who was also in her freshman year. Her interests are mainly in quantum physics and astronomy, and they'd set up for hours talking about new discoveries in all areas of physics.

Their friendship remained strong throughout their respective college careers, and they would sit outside for many a night talking about the cosmos and, occasionally, about who the cutest guy on campus might be. During their graduate studies, they found that they'd taken some of the same classes and when they wrote term papers, they often critiqued each other's work. Then the day came – graduation. Both Catherine and Nancy were receiving their Ph.D. degrees, and there were many congratulatory handshakes and pictures to be taken. Catherine had her picture taken with her parents, William and Emily, and Nancy was glad to stand in as the photographer. Catherine made it a point to have her picture taken with just her father, and it was this photograph that she would come to treasure. When the pictures came back, her father signed that one particular photograph for her, 'Congratulations Cat! Love, Dad'.

Shortly after graduation, Catherine was offered a professor position at Bowdoin, and she accepted this full-time post as Dr. Catherine Thomaston, professor of theoretical physics. Later, after running into Nancy again, Catherine found out that she too had accepted a professor position, teaching quantum physics at the graduate level. They both gave each other a celebratory hug and decided that a girl's night out was in order. But, they promised each other not to drink too much. Mostly for safety, but they also had one other consideration in mind. No one can teach physics while hung over and feeling the urge to puke. After their night out, they each got back to their respective apartments. But, morning came with the screaming fire of sunlight shining through their windows and piercing are slightly numbed brains. They ran into each other at the student center the next day, with Nancy wearing sunglasses.

"I feel like shit," Nancy quietly said.

"Let me see the eyes," Catherine said with a grin.

Nancy lowered her sunglasses enough for Catherine to see the circles that seemed to cradle her bloodshot eyes.

"Jesus Christ!" Catherine exclaimed. "You look like shit!"

Nancy was not amused.

"But in a good way," Catherine said, comically.

She giggled a bit at Nancy's expense, then, both started quietly laughing.

"I don't think I'll be doing that again for a long time," Nancy proclaimed.

"Good," Catherine replied with a smirk. "Because you do look like shit."


Catherine jumped into her new career with both feet. Teaching gave her great satisfaction, knowing that she was contributing to the growth of some of the brightest minds in the country. She knew how much work went into the program, as well as the amount of discipline it required. So, she gave each student the respect they deserved for putting their lives aside for the sake of studying a very complex subject.


A year later, her father, William, was diagnosed with a heart condition. It wasn't serious, but it did require a regimen of blood-thinning medications in order to minimize the formation of blood clots. He would take them indefinitely. His doctor at Franklin Memorial wanted him to go to

Portland for a complete cardiac workup. William sighed a bit.

"Could this get worse?" he asked.

"You might be able to live with this, as it is right now, for the rest of your life," the doctor said. "Or things could change. There is still the risk that you might develop a clot, and no one can predict where it will go. That's why I want you to get the workup done. We need to take a look at the bigger picture."

After arriving at Maine Medical Center with Emily and going through the admission process, he was scheduled for a stress test. This would be the first of many tests he would undergo during the diagnostic process, and he was young enough that he could use their treadmill. But during the test, the doctors noticed a significant change in Williams's EKG. They stopped the treadmill and asked him how he was feeling.

"Kind of sick to my stomach," he answered. They had him sit in a chair while continuing to monitor his vital signs. And while checking his blood pressure, he broke into a heavy sweat as his EKG changed again – this time into a dangerous arrhythmia. Suddenly, his face grew pale as his eyes widened, and his pupils became dilated. His body went limp as he slumped over to one side and was caught by the doctors, who lowered him to the floor. A team of doctors and nurses immediately flooded the room and quickly assessed his condition. It became necessary to place a breathing tube down his throat while cardiac drugs were being pushed into his veins. Defibrillator pads were applied to his chest and back. In order to synchronize the muscles in his heart and bring it back to a normal rhythm, a sudden shock of electricity was delivered through the pads. William's body flinched slightly, but the doctors had successfully brought him back from the brink of death. He was transferred immediately to the cardiac intensive care unit, where he was placed in a bed it was routinely left available and commonly referred to as a 'code bed'. While the nurses and technicians moved William into the room with the machinery that would keep him alive, Emily was brought to the unit and the doctors reviewed his condition with her. Emily asked to use the nearest phone and immediately dialed Catherine's number. After her phone rang a few times, her answering machine picked up. "Dammit, where is she," she said, hanging up the phone.

She looked over at the clock, which read 2:30 -- Catherine would be in class. Emily hated the idea of having to call her while she was working, but this was important. Her father could be dying. So, Emily called the Dean at Bowdoin College, who went directly to the lecture hall where Catherine was in the middle of discussing Einstein's time paradox. He motioned to her from the back of the room.

"Okay, everyone," she said to her students. "Let's take a quick break."
She approached the Dean without saying a word, as though she knew that something bad had happened.

"Hi, Catherine," he said. His voice was sensitive and caring. This made her feel even more uncomfortable.

"I just got off the phone with your mother. Your father's at Maine Medical Center." Catherine suddenly brought her hands up to her mouth and her eyes widened with fear.

"I don't have any details about this, but your mom sounds scared, and I think you should be there for her. I'll let your class out early."
Without so much as a word, she ran out to her car and started towards Portland, and an hour later was pulling into the visitor parking lot. She pushed through the revolving doors, went to the front desk, and asked what room he was in.

"He's in cardiac intensive care on the ninth floor," the woman at the desk said.
She ran down the hallway and past the lab, where she immediately found herself confused by the busyness and size of the hospital. And as she began looking for any signs that might direct her, a voice called to her from behind.

"Excuse me, are you lost?"
Catherine spun around to face a man dressed in a white lab coat, pushing a black cart holding a red

box containing everything needed for the purpose of drawing blood.

"Yes!" she replied. "I need to get to the cardiac intensive care unit."

"Sure, I'm going in that direction. I'll get you there," he said.
The man seemed to be in his 40s -- bald, with a gray goatee, wearing glasses and a gentle, patient smile. He walked Catherine down just beyond a blue wall at the end of the hallway and escorted her into an elevator. Pushing the buttons for the fifth and ninth floors, he turned back to her. "You want to get off on the ninth floor, go to the desk and the nurses can show you where you need to go."

"Thank you very much," she said.

"You'revery welcome," he replied.

"Here's my stop."
The elevator opened its doors at the fifth floor, and he stepped out, disappearing down the hallway. The doors closed as the elevator continued up to the ninth floor. When they opened again, Catherine walked out and immediately found her way to the desk. She walked up and asked a rather young, blond-haired nurse where the cardiac intensive care unit was.

"Right down there," she said, pointing down to a set of ominous-looking double doors. The doors automatically opened and she walked in. One look around led Catherine into a state of emotional disbelief. She had never seen people in this state, with wires and tubes everywhere and machines breathing for those being kept in medically induced comas -- their lungs were routinely being suctioned out. There were banks of monitoring machines in every room that would alarm at the smallest deviation from what was considered stable. To Catherine, it looked more like a warehouse than a hospital, and this left her feeling more than a bit unsettled.

"Can I help you?" a woman's voice asked. She turned to face the voice.

"Uh… yes. I'm looking for William Thomason. I was told he was here," she said cautiously, hoping that he might be elsewhere in the hospital -- somewhere where death might not be hiding.

"He's right down in the room on the end," the woman said. "I can take you down there."

"Thank you," Catherine said.
She was led down to the room where her father was and when the curtains were pulled back, Catherine's heart sank as her fears rose. She felt a strange, cold sensation in her stomach as her thoughts started to become a bit muddied. Catherine walked into the room and with tears welling up in her eyes, she gently approached the side of her father's bed.

"Daddy, it's me, Cat," she said.
She picked up his hand, only to realize that he was both cold and somewhat stiff.

"Catherine?"

It was her mother. Her face was flushed, and her eyes were red with tears flowing down her cheeks. She walked over to Catherine and slowly put her arms around her waist. She was without words and simply cried on Catherine's blouse for what seemed like forever.

"Mom, the doctors are going to do everything they can," she said, trying to be reassuring. "Are you the family?" Both women turned toward the voice coming from the foot of the bed.

"Hi, I'm Dr. Hanscom. I'm the resident in charge of Mr. Thomaston's care."
He seemed to be in his late 20s, with a very professional demeanor.

"I'll need to ask you a few questions about his health. We already have faxed records from his doctor at Franklin Memorial, but there are still some questions we always ask the family."
There was about a 10-minute exchange of questions and answers -- mostly yes or no questions.

"So, what can you tell us?" Catherine asked. Her mother had moved to the head of the bed, where she began talking to William with the hope that he could somehow hear her.

"Well, according to the report from the beginning of his cardiac workup, his heart went into an arrhythmia. He lost consciousness and was resuscitated," he said. "We're still assessing how much damage may have been done to his heart muscle and will be getting him into the cardiac

catheterization lab within the next 15 minutes. After that, we'll have a much better idea about what's going on."
Emily then spoke up.

"I don't understand. His doctor put him on blood thinners last week. I thought those drugs were supposed to keep things like this from happening."

"Ordinarily, they do," the doctor said. "But, it takes time for them to reach a level where they become effective. Right now, he's on a heparin drip and that will keep any further clots from forming."

"I have a question, doctor," Catherine said. "Why is he so cold? Shouldn't he have some blankets over him?"

"That's a good question," the doctor replied. "One of the things we can do to treat it as a particular condition is called 'therapeutic hypothermia'. We use medication to stabilize the metabolism, and we bring the body's temperature down. This allows the body to redirect all of its energy into the healing process."

"Can he hear us?" asked Emily.

"Well, he's pretty sedated right now," he said. "But, some people believe that even under sedation, some patients might be able to hear on a subconscious level. Now, just in case, if something happens, and he needs to be resuscitated again, what would you like us to do?"

"What do you mean?" Catherine asked.

"Do you want us to try and bring him back?"
he replied.
Catherine and Emily turned to each other rather
dumbfoundedly.
"Let's do this. Let's see what the cardiac
catheterization results and the blood work say,
and will touch back on this issue later. Sound like
a plan?"
Both women nodded their heads.
"Okay," they agreed.
They both stepped out of the room as the bed and
equipment were slowly moved out and down the
hall to the cardiac catheterization lab. It would
take 30 minutes to an hour before the procedure
was finished. In the meantime, Catherine and her
mother were shown to the waiting room. At some
point, Emily broke the silence that had so heavily
filled the room.
"Did you call Robert?" she asked.
Robert was living in Washington State and was
not the most pleasant person to deal with. As a
boy, he was always off by himself. Eventually, he
would come to resent Catherine for the attention
she received from their father, as well as his
father. But, he would never learn that a parent
can't provide attention to someone who isn't there
to receive it, and over the years, his hostility
would only grow. Catherine always suspected that
this was probably why he moved to the other side
of the country.

Catherine stepped out near the elevators and turned on her cell phone. After getting a signal, she brought his number up from her contacts list. She stared at it for a few seconds and became aware that if it were not for their father's condition, she would probably never hear his voice again. She also realized how terrible it felt to be written off, a member of her own family. Catherine took a deep breath and prepared herself for what she knew would be a hostile conversation. She dialed the number, hoping Robert was out -- after all, there were four time zones difference between Maine and Washington State.

"Hello." His voice sounded distant and oddly warm.

"Robert, it's Catherine," she said. There was a brief pause.

"What, did someone die?" he asked sarcastically.
Catherine took another deep breath, trying to remain composed.

"Robert, dad had a heart attack," she said.

"What do you want me to do about it?" he said.

"Look, we don't know how bad this could get," Catherine said. "I thought it might be important for you to be here, and mom's a wreck."

"Well, I'm afraid I can't make things any better," Roberts said.

His voice was distant and hostile. Catherine was expecting this but held out a little hope that maybe he would care about how their mother was doing.

"And since you're there, you can handle mom."

"Jesus fucking Christ, Robert!" Catherine said, with increasing agitation.

"He's your father! He's been a model father to both of us!"

"Well," he replied, with obvious sarcasm. "I guess that'd be true coming from daddy's little girl."

"God dammit!" She said.
Catherine could no longer hold back her anger.

"Don't start this shit! Good God! And you're a psychologist?!"

"Hey!" he said. "I don't get paid to give a shit! I wanted to go into research, not listen to people's pathetic little problems."

"Fine, whatever," Catherine replied. "That's your issue! Are you going to be here or not? This may be the last chance you have to see him."
She heard an impatient sigh over the phone.

"You handle it!" he said.
Robert's hostility had not abated in the slightest.

"Alright, fine!" Catherine said, with a noticeable touch of sarcasm.

"So, if dad dies, are you even going to bother to show up at the God damned funeral?"
This question was met with a pause, then the line went dead.

"Robert?!"

Catherine cursed under her breath as she dialed his number again.

"Son of a bitch…"

She let the line ring until his answering machine picked up and when she heard the recorded message, hung up and turned her phone off. She was struck with the pain of knowing that her family was irreparably fractured, but also with the realization that their mother would probably never see him again. Catherine backed up against the wall and brought her hands over her face.

"You fucking bastard," she said, while quietly weeping.

"Catherine?" It was her mother. "Is Robert coming?"

"Uh… he can't, mom," Catherine answered. "One of his patients is in trouble and he sort of has to be there."

Her lie was well-meaning but obvious to her mother.

"Catherine," Emily said, with a gentle tone. "You're such a terrible liar. Come on, we'll get through this."

They walked slowly back to the cardiac intensive care unit just as William was being moved back from the catheterization Lab. When the nurses finished moving the bed and machinery back into the room, they once again returned to his bedside. About 10 minutes later, the doctor returned with Williams's chart.

"Well, we got the report back from the catheterization lab," he said.
Catherine and Emily stood momentarily with their eyes widened in anticipation of what might be the worst possible news.

"I just wish I had better news for you. According to the results of his catheterization, and his lab results, William has about 20% heart functioning. They were able to remove a blood clot from one of the arteries in his heart, but this kind of damage can't be reversed." Catherine and her mother remained wide-eyed with shock and disbelief.

"I'm sorry," Dr. Hanscom continued. "I wish there was something we could do. At this point, all we can do is to make him comfortable. Usually, we ask the family what they want us to do in case the patient's heart stops, but I think that decision's already been made for us."

"So, what now?" Catherine asked, with tears streaming down her face.
Emily was at his head again, talking to him quietly -- saying her goodbyes.

"I think what we can expect is a steady decline of functioning. This could take a few hours, or it could take a day or more," he replied. "Are they are any other family members who might want to be here?"

"Uh, no," Catherine said, with a flat tone.

"Alright," the doctor responded. "If you need anything, the nurses are right here and if you need to take a break, the waiting room is right around the corner." "Thank you," Catherine said quietly.

"Could we get a couple of chairs?" she asked.

"Absolutely," he said.

Within minutes, two chairs were brought into the room, and they sat in quiet vigilance as William slowly slipped away. And within four hours, the machines were turned off, leaving Catherine and her mother sitting in the dim light, saying their final goodbyes. They left the room and sat with each other in the waiting room. Catherine couldn't believe how something like this could happen so quickly, but she also felt comforted but the fact that her father didn't suffer. Emily slowly looked up at her and said, "What am I going to do without your father?"

She then quickly became inconsolable.

Three days later, Catherine found herself sitting in the front row at a funeral home in Farmington. On one side sat her mother, who was gently rocking back and forth, while quietly weeping. On the other, lay an open casket containing the body of her father. The room was filled with people, mostly from the college, and more were filing past the casket. Some remarked on how suddenly his death had occurred, while others commented on how good he looked. Robert had been e-mailed about the funeral, as he was not answering his phone. But, at no time during the service was there any sign of him. The eulogy was delivered by a local pastor and ran for about 20 minutes. But, for Catherine, most of it was a blur. During the wake, most people expressed both sympathy and support, while a few remained a bit distant, seemingly at a loss for words. Over the next two weeks, there were many phone conversations between Catherine and her mother. Emily would routinely call her out of loneliness. She didn't seem to know what to do with herself with William gone. Eventually, Catherine talked her into joining a support group, where she began making some friends. And, during those times when it was her turn to host the group's meetings, she fell into the role of hostess with great ease. Catherine was very relieved to see her acquiring friends and knew that without emotional support, her mother would undoubtedly slip into a depression. Catherine, on the other hand, was keenly aware that she was not handling her father's death very well at all. She missed him constantly, sometimes breaking into tears. Occasionally, she would be forced into letting a class out early when her emotions began to overtake her. She would often rely on Nancy for support.

"I miss my dad so much," she'd cry.

"Listen, sweetie," Nancy said with a caring voice. "I can't tell you that you'll get over this. This kind of thing stays with you forever. But, I can tell you that things will get better and the days

will get easier. After a few months, you'll be back to your old self."
But this would not be the case for Catherine, as several months went by and her grief had not lessened, seemingly in the slightest. Nancy stepped in again -- this time, to get Catherine into counseling.

"Cat, people are talking," Nancy said. "You're letting classes out early, and sometimes you're there late. You're becoming disorganized and people are noticing that you're losing weight. People are starting to think you're sick -- really sick!"
Catherine came to see Nancy as her rock, but there was only so much she could do, even as a friend. And Nancy quickly realized that Catherine would get help only if she wanted to. So, she began thinking about how to get her to the realization that she both needed and wanted to get help. The next day, Nancy made a visit to Catherine's office.

"Knock, knock," she said while standing at the open door.

"Hey, come on in," Catherine said, as she threw some tissue in a wastebasket.
Her eyes were a bit red, and she was sniffling as though she'd been crying. Nancy sat in the chair next to Catherine's desk and closed the door.

"What's up?" Catherine asked.

"We need to talk, Cath," Nancy said.
Her tone started to become serious.

"Cath, the chair of the department came to my office yesterday asking about you. He wanted to know if I thought you were stable enough to continue teaching. I told him yes. If the head of the department is asking questions, that's a big deal!" Catherine sat, eyes glazed with anxiety over the sudden possibility that she could lose her job. She loved teaching and considered it her life's work -- her mission.

"I know I'm having some issues right now, but I'll be okay," Catherine said.
She was near complete denial.

"Cath, this is Dr. Warner, the chair of the department," Nancy said, as she took Catherine's hand in order to get her full attention.

"He's starting to wonder about your state of mind, and he may be starting to doubt your competency as a teacher. Cath, you're going to be considered for tenure in six months, and you love teaching. So, don't tell me that you'll be okay. Do you really believe that you'll be okay?"
Catherine slid back into her chair as Nancy slightly tightened her grip.

"I don't know," she said, with a deep sigh. "It's been so long since I actually had a good day… and sometimes I just can't think straight. Jesus Christ… what the fuck is wrong with me?!"

"Cath," Nancy said.
Her voice was caring, but still very concerned. "If they think that you're no longer able to teach, they're going to cut you loose. Now, ask yourself

this: what else could you do besides teach? Research jobs are very rare -- you know that. And I don't want to see you, with a Ph.D., ending up as a fucking greeter in some piss-ant little tourist trap somewhere. And denial is only going to get you there faster."

"I just don't know what to do!" Catherine said, with a hopeless tone in her voice.
Nancy handed her a piece of paper with a phone number written on it.

"This is the number for a grief counselor," she said. "If you want me to go with you, I will. But, you have to do this. We're talking about your career, and teaching is your life. I'm afraid of what could happen to you if they let you go. Cath, please call them."
They met after classes let out for the day and went back to Catherine's apartment. Nancy sat with her while she dialed the number on the piece of paper.

"Franklin Memorial medical arts," a female voice answered.

"Yeah, hi," Catherine said. "I'm looking for the grief counseling office."

"Okay, one moment," the voice said. There was a pause and a line began to ring again. A different voice answered this time.

"Dr. Howard Beach, can I help you?"
Catherine described her problem and gave the woman her name, address, and phone number, then an initial appointment was set up. She hung

up the phone after writing down the appointment date and time. Nancy put a hand on her arm.

"Doing okay?" she asked.

"Actually, I feel a bit relieved," Catherine replied.

"That's good!" Nancy said. "You need to do this."

"I know," said Catherine. "If I can't save my sanity, everything else is going to go to shit."

Catherine went to her weekly appointments religiously and within six months, her life seemed to be back on track. Then, during a girls' night out, Nancy asked her a question she hadn't expected.

"So, now that things are going better, have you been giving any thought to, uh…you know?" Nancy asked, teasingly.
After a moment, it finally dawned on Catherine as to what she was talking about.

"Oh, I don't know," she said. "I think I'm finally coming to terms with everything and I don't want to complicate my life… just yet. I just don't think I'm ready to start dating just yet."

"Okay, fair enough," Nancy replied. "But, when you get to that point, I can set you up with a really nice guy."

"Well," Catherine said. "When I'm ready – but, we double-date. It'll take some of the pressure off."

"Agreed," said Nancy, with a grin.

Catherine continued teaching, and she felt each day get a bit easier to deal with. Her thinking became clearer and soon her mind was once again moving at near-light speed with ideas, equations, and solutions. Three months later, she felt like she was at the top of her game and the department chair started talking about tenure. But, in spite of her recovery, Catherine would occasionally feel some small part of something twinge deeply inside her. It felt a small pin prick touching her inside, that place that seemed vague and indiscriminate. Nancy told her that even though she was doing well, she would always carry a small spot of pain around inside her, but even that would fade over time. Catherine came to the conclusion that it made sense and blew it off is a necessary part of the healing process.

Over the next month, she started to feel uneasy when she began to notice that those feelings had not changed. In fact, they were becoming more frequent, and she was beginning to experience some degree of agitation. Not long after this, Nancy caught up to her in the hallway between classes.

"Hey, Cath," she said. "How about a girls' night out this Friday?"
Catherine stopped and turned towards her. She was clutching her books and notes tightly against her chest, and Nancy immediately noticed that she seemed unusually stressed. There was always a lot

of work to do during midterms, but that was why professors had teaching assistants. And it didn't explain Catherine's general appearance and her change of mood.

"I… I don't really feel like it," she said. "I haven't been feeling well lately."

"Is there anything I can do?" Nancy asked.

"Look!" Catherine said.

Her voice became somewhat defensive.

"I just don't feel like it."

She turned away from Nancy and quickly continued down the hallway.

Nancy was left in a state of shock and concern. She wanted to know what was happening to her friend. They had been like sisters for a very long time, and she knew that something was terribly wrong. Suddenly, she realized who might be able to help, and she turned to Frederick Markley. Dr. Markley, as he preferred to be called, was the chair of the psychology department. He was a brilliant man who had organized and directed most of the studies carried out by the Defense Department, regarding the psyche's response to battle. This included the conflict between training and the need to survive under combat conditions.

Nancy stepped up to his office door and knocked politely.

"Dr. Markley?" she said.

He looked up at Nancy over his reading glasses, taking his eyes up from the minutes of a recent department meeting.

"Hi, I'm Nancy, Professor of quantum physics. I called earlier to get a few minutes of your time."

"Yes, come in," he said. "So, doctor, what can I do for you?"

Nancy sat down and described Catherine's behavior as accurately as she could, and mentioned the recent passing of her father as well.

"Honestly," Dr. Markley said. "I'm not a clinician, but it sounds like your friend is headed for some serious trouble. Agitation can be a symptom of a few different things – paranoia, depression, bipolar disorder, schizophrenia, and even one or two personality disorders. Without the onset of symptoms that would be specific to a certain illness, it's hard for me to put a finger on one issue. Has she seen a therapist?"

"When she was in grief counseling, she was seeing a psychiatrist," Nancy replied.

"Well," he said. "I think you should get her to go back."

Nancy nodded her head in discouragement.

"I'm sorry I can't tell you more."

They shook hands as Nancy thanked him for his time, and she walked out feeling rather helpless. As she left the building, she was suddenly struck by a feeling of urgency that she couldn't explain. Somehow, she knew that Catherine was in trouble and ran to her office, where she found Catherine in the middle of an anxiety attack.

"Cath, what's wrong?" Nancy said, trying to sound calm.

"I don't know!" She replied. "I can't stop it! I think I'm dying!"

"Cath, you're not dying," said Nancy.

"You're having an anxiety attack."

"It won't leave me alone," she said.

"What won't leave you alone?" Nancy asked.

"I don't know… it's always there – inside me," said Catherine.
She was terrified of something vague – something she felt, but couldn't understand.

"I think it wants something, but I don't know what it is!"
Nancy gently took her by the shoulder, turning her around, so they sat face-to-face. "Cath, listen to me," Nancy said firmly. "I don't know what's going on, but we have to figure this out, and I'm not going to leave you alone with this. Now, I'm taking you to the hospital. I'll have your teaching assistant take your classes, and I'll tell Dr. Warner that you have the flu."

After visiting the emergency room, the doctor prescribed an antidepressant and an antianxiety drug. He also recommended that Catherine take about a week off from work to get a break from the stress of the job. He faxed her records onto Dr. Beach, Catherine's psychiatrist, and told her that she was to follow up with him. When she got home, Catherine made the appointment, and a week later, she felt well enough to return to work. As the days passed, she began to feel somewhat distracted and over the following week, she again started to become agitated. She hadn't seen Nancy in a couple of days, and the antianxiety pills only made her drowsy. But beyond that, they didn't seem to be working.

Then, one afternoon, while teaching, she heard a whisper from among her class. She turned around toward her students and searched through their faces.

"Questions anyone?" she asked.
There was no response, so she turned back to the board and continued. Again, she heard a whisper, but this time it seemed to be coming from directly behind her, and for one brief instant she was able to focus her attention on it. It didn't seem to say anything that made sense and, in fact, sounded very nondescript – almost like a voice, but not sounding like anything she'd ever heard before. And when she heard it a third time, it seemed to be a bit louder. Catherine was suddenly overtaken with panic and dropped her chalk to the floor as she was momentarily frozen where she stood. She managed to force herself to turn around toward the class again, composing herself enough to release her students early.

"Sorry, everyone," she said. "I've had the flu for a couple of days, and I'm suddenly not feeling well."

After the students left, Catherine sat down in the front row and tried to compose herself when she heard the sound again. This time, not only did it still seem to be coming from behind her, but it was now clearer. Now, she heard only a single word – her name. She bolted up out of the chair and looked around the room.

"Who's there!" she yelled. "This isn't funny! I'm calling campus security!" Catherine didn't know the number, but she wanted to sound threatening. She was alone, but still felt very uneasy and agitated. She quickly picked up her books and left the classroom. But as she began to pass through the doorway, she was compelled to turn her head back slightly. And through the corner of her eye, she glimpsed what appeared to be a male figure sitting in the exact chair she had occupied just moments ago. The figure was looking at her with a slight grin, and Catherine slammed the door shut. Running to her office, she locked the door behind her and sat on the floor, against the wall, watching the door in terror. After a few minutes, she saw a shadow down the hall through the frosted glass of her office door. She sat on the floor in terrified stillness, while the shadow inched closer to the door. Her knees came up to the fetal position as she covered her eyes – half crying, half hyperventilating. When Catherine brought her head back up, the shadow was gone and all she heard was her heart pounding in her ears. Crawling over to her desk, she grabbed her keys and arranged them between the fingers of her closed fist. And as she quickly walked to the door, she brought her fist up to her shoulder, with her elbow pulled back slightly.

"Don't fuck with me," she whispered. "Don't fuck…with…me!"

She threw the door open and lunged into the hallway, only to find it empty. In a state of paranoia, Catherine slid down the side of the metal door frame, putting her hands on the floor. She began crawling around the hallways, trying to find this person before they found her.

"Where are you? You son of a bitch," she muttered.

She looked carefully around corners and through the windows of office doors. "Catherine?" a voice came from behind her.

It was the head of the department, and he had no idea of what Catherine was now capable of.

"Catherine, what's wrong?"

She backed herself into a corner, looking up at him as though she'd become possessed by a wildcat. Her hair had become disheveled, and she'd broken into a heavy sweat, with the single thought that her life was in immediate danger.

"What do you want from me?" she screamed. "Don't touch me! I swear to God, I'll fucking kill you!"

She held up her fist, still with fingers interlaced with keys.

"I mean it!" she screamed, once again. Hearing this chaos, the department secretary came running down. The department head held a hand out to her and quietly told her to call 911. The secretary disappeared and within five minutes, the sound of sirens could be heard rapidly approaching the building.

As the ambulance pulled up in front of the building, Dr. Warner carefully stepped toward Catherine, partly to comfort her and partly to help her feel in control, making it easier for her to get into the ambulance. His actions were well intended, but she got to her feet as she steps forward. And in a delusional moment of panic, Catherine threw her key-laden fist out, striking him across the left side of his face. The impact grayed his vision slightly and tore the side of his face down to the bone. Blood poured out of the deep, gaping wound as he staggered back to the wall. He put a hand up to his face and stared in shock at the amount of blood that covered it, as he slid down the wall into a sitting position. The force of Catherine's swing left blood spattered on the wall, as well as a heavy trail of drops on the floor that followed Dr. Warner to where he sat. The paramedics appeared in the hallway with two police officers closely following behind, just as Catherine charged at him for a second assault. She was immediately restrained by the officers, while one of the paramedics went to retrieve a gurney and the other radioed to the hospital that they were bringing in a violent patient. Catherine was wrestled down to the gurney and restrained by her wrists and ankles with heavy canvas straps. Screaming the entire way to the hospital, she continued to make wild accusations about being followed through the hallways, as well is the claim that Dr. Warner tried to rape her.

"He fucking got what he deserved, that son of a bitch!" she screamed.

She was wheeled into the emergency room, still screaming about being followed.

"What do they want from me?!" she asked beggingly. "You know what they want? I know what they want. They want to get inside me. They're already in my head! Get them out!" she cried.

"Please, make them get out!"

One moment, Catherine was pleading for help. The next, she was making violent accusations toward whoever happened to be near her.

The doctor in charge of the emergency room was trying to assess Catherine's condition when Nancy ran in. She followed the sound of screaming, assuming that it was Catherine. When she entered the room, a nurse was attempting to calm her down, while the doctor was preparing a mild sedative for injection. As soon as she saw Nancy, Catherine began crying.

"Nancy?" she asked.

"I'm right here, sweetie," Nancy replied.

"Please make them get out," Catherine begged. "Please!"

"Cath," Nancy said, trying to be reassuring. "The doctors are going to do everything they can, alright? They're all here to help you."

"No," Catherine said suspiciously.

"They killed daddy! And now, they're going to kill me!"
She started to become more agitated.

"They've been following me at work! You have to stop them!"
Nancy looked up hopelessly at the doctor as he injected Catherine with the sedative -- 2 milliliters of Lorazepam. And after about 10 minutes, she fell into a calm, drug-induced sleep. The doctor looked up at Nancy with a deep sigh of relief.

"So, are you family?" he asked.
Nancy's eyes welled up with tears.

"No," she said. "But we're like sisters, and her mom is way up in Farmington."

"Can you answer a few questions about her?" the doctor asked.

"Yeah," she replied. "I'll do my best."
They both went into a small room designated for the families of patients, where about a 10-minute exchange of questions and answers took place.

The psychiatrist on call was consulted and Catherine's doctor was notified of her condition.

After the two had conferred with each other, it was decided that Catherine would be admitted to the hospital's psychiatric unit for a more in-depth assessment. The next day, her psychiatrist, Dr. Beach, made a visit in order to make an assessment. A few minutes later, Nancy arrived, asking if she could visit. She was told that it was too soon for Catherine to be getting visitors, as she was not yet stable and many things needed to be addressed. Nancy gave them her phone number and asked that she be called when Catherine was able to receive visitors. Nancy had also been keeping Catherine's mother up to date as to what had happened and promised to continue doing so. That evening, Catherine was started on an antipsychotic drug called Haloperidol. At first, she violently refused it, claiming that the doctors were trying to kill her. The doctor in charge of her case finally resorted to an intramuscular injection of the drug and within 15 minutes, Catherine became drowsy from its effects. A few hours later, she woke with a foggy recollection of some of the events that led to her admission. At first, she begged to go home, threatening to call a lawyer and personally sue her doctor for false imprisonment. But, after a nurse sat down with her and prompted Catherine to reflect on the previous events, she came to realize that she desperately needed help, if she was going to get her life back.

She began an intensive one-week inpatient program of daily therapy sessions and medication management. And while it was agreed that Catherine was making some limited progress, it was also agreed that she needed more treatment than the one-week program could provide. So, Catherine would be transferred to the Augusta Mental Health Institute for their one-month treatment program. When Catherine was informed of this part of the treatment plan, she understood enough to be terrified.

"Please don't lock me away in there!" she begged. "I'll die in that place!"
She was reassured by the nurse that this would not be the case and that AMHI had a very successful treatment rate. But, in Catherine's still delusional mind, she felt as though the world was coming to an end and that she would never again see the light of day.

Once she was admitted, Catherine was taken to her room. It was fairly small, with only a hospital bed in a small dresser. She walked slowly into the adjoining bathroom to relieve herself and noticed the absence of a mirror. It was then she realized how serious things had become when it dawned on her that it had been removed in order to prevent the glass from being used as a method of suicide. After leaving the bathroom, Catherine slowly walked out of the room and down the hallway. Her thinking was still foggy from the effect of the haloperidol injections, but she thought it was important to become familiar with her temporary home. She walked past the nurse's desk but had not noticed the vigilant glance they gave her. One of them opened her chart in order to become more familiar with her case. The nurse noticed immediately that a red sticker had been placed on the history page, denoting a violent and potentially dangerous patient.

Catherine walked down toward the end of the hallway when she suddenly found herself enveloped in an ear-shattering silence. She quickly looked around the now empty hallway -- there were no nurses, no patients. Catherine found herself frighteningly alone, dressed only in a hospital gown and walking in bare feet. She turned back toward the end of the hallway, having become startled by something within the silence. A white light shone furiously through a large window ahead of her, and she heard a tapping sound echo through the hallway. The sound grabbed her curiosity and pulled her towards the window. As Catherine passed the room's entrance, she noticed a sign on the door – 'Transorbital Suite'. She was not familiar with the word transorbital and her curiosity piqued. When she stepped in front of the window, her eyes were momentarily bleached by the light that seemed to explode from within the room. Her eyes opened wide with horror as they adjusted to the light, her mouth falling open in disbelief. A team of gowned doctors and nurses were gathered around a patient who lay naked on a surgical table. The caps and masks they wore left them unrecognizable and seemingly devoid of anything that could be thought of as human, as they stood fixed in place with their gloved hands held up near their shoulders.

Catherine saw a doctor holding a long, thin instrument between the patient's eye and eye socket, while methodically and slowly advancing it into their brain with a stainless steel mallet. After the mallet was placed on a nearby tray, the faceless doctor wrapped his index finger around the far end of the protruding instrument and firmly pulled it up over the patient's forehead. With this single act, Catherine gasped audibly while bringing her hands to her mouth. And when the doctors and nurses simultaneously turned and fixed their unblinking eyes on her, she became frozen with fear. Moments later, the patient, with the instrument still fixed in their eye socket, slowly sat up and fixed his gaze on her as well. Her emotions slammed Catherine back against the wall behind her as her attention was dragged to the patient's eye, which had become partially pushed out of its socket from the pressure of the instrument that was being used to perform a procedure sometimes referred to as an 'ice pick lobotomy'. With both hands over her mouth, she turned her back toward the hallway she had entered from and as Catherine began to scream, a pair of muscular arms surrounded her from behind.

"Catherine," the voice said. "You're not supposed to be down here. Didn't they tell you that bad things happen down here?"

"Let go of me!" Catherine screamed.

"Oh, not just yet, Cat," the voice replied. "Let's have some fun first."

Catherine glanced over to one side and noticed the shoulder of a hospital scrub shirt, as the man quickly slipped a hand over her breast.

"You piece of shit!" she screamed.

"Oh, now come on, doesn't that feel better, Cat?" the voice replied.

Catherine slid her hands around behind her, grabbing the faceless man by the testicles, and drove her nails into them. As he screamed and bent down toward the floor, Catherine met him halfway with her knee, planting it violently in the middle of his face. And in the ferocity of her attack, she heard the snap of breaking cartilage as she made contact, leaving blood drops on the front of her gown. Catherine broke away from his grasp, still never having seen his face, and ran down the still empty hallway towards the locked door that lay as the line between freedom and the terrors of psychiatric incarceration. She fell against the metal door, screaming and demanding to be let out. She was immediately confronted by a nurse, who firmly spun her around in order to speak with her face to face. Catherine was now looking down the hallway once again, which lay in front of her bustling with the activities of nurses and other patients -- some wandering aimlessly while others simply walked in circles.

"Catherine," the nurse said. "You're not supposed to go off on your own."
Catherine was dumbstruck.

"Can you walk with me?" she asked. "I need to show you something."

"Of course," the nurse replied.
They walked together down to the far end of the hall to the window.

"What is it, Catherine?" asked the nurse.

"It was here! They were all here -- in that room," she replied.

"And there was a guy on the table with something like a long nail sticking out of his eye and a doctor pounding it into his head."
But the room was bare, and the equipment lay long overdue for cleaning. Catherine stepped up to the glass and realized how much of the tiled walls had begun to chip and fall off. The room looked as though it hadn't been used for decades.

"I think we should get you back to your room -- you look very tired," the nurse said.

Catherine realized that a moment ago, the entire unit was empty, except for the doctors performing the lobotomy and the man that assaulted her. Of course, he was nowhere to be found, and the procedure room now lay in ruins. The nurse walks Catherine slowly back to her room and helped her lie down on the bed. She had now reached the full realization of the seriousness of her illness. She knew that her future would offer good days and bad days. But more painfully, Catherine realized that she would never be able to go back to complete sanity and that she would never again be the person she once was. During the next week, she was placed on a second antipsychotic drug. It was thought that the second medication would treat those features of her illness that the haloperidol alone could not. With this new combination, Catherine began experiencing more mental clarity and having better days in general. However, she occasionally would walk down to the end of the hallway where the procedure room was and simply stare at it.

"It was so real," she thought out loud. She shuddered in horror as she recalled the naked man sitting up, looking at her with one eye as the other had been pushed over by a tool that looked very much like an ice pick. In talking about these things with the staff psychiatrist, it was concluded that Catherine was now in a place where she was beginning to realize reality from her hallucinations. Over the following week, the medications gradually took a stronger hold on her mental state as her thinking, once again, became lucid. The only drawback seems to be a few side effects – a lack of concentration, as well as some short-term memory loss, seemed to be the most annoying.

Catherine was released by the end of the following week. Nancy thought it might be a good idea if she moved in with her for a couple of weeks so that Catherine wouldn't have to be alone. She arranged two more weeks of leave time with Bowdoin in order to regain her center. Thirty days in a psychiatric hospital had turned out to be quite traumatic, and Catherine needed the rest. However, during this time she went to see Dr. Warner. She was able to recover some degree of the events that took place during her initial breakdown in the hallway and was very anxious about meeting with him. But, she knew that this day would come and if she was to return to teaching, she would have to face him. Catherine quietly walked into Dr. Warner's office without having made an appointment and tapped on the door. As he looked up from his desk, he smiled broadly.

"Catherine!" he said. "It's good to see you!" She was shocked to hear such a pleasant tone coming from someone who had, only a few weeks ago, ended up at the business end of a fistful of keys, being swung by someone who was dangerously psychotic. Dr. Warner motioned her to a chair in front of his desk. The side of his face looked like he'd had many stitches recently removed. But, it was quite difficult to see his wounds, as he had started growing a beard in order to cover them.

"Uh… Dr. Warner… I," she started.

"Catherine," he said. "It's okay. I can't say that I know how you feel and honestly, I hope I never do. But, don't worry about it. Besides, my wife thinks the beard looks pretty good and the doctor said there was no permanent damage. So, it'll be just a couple of scars and that's not a big deal." Catherine expressed an audible sigh of relief, believing that anyone else would have fired her or, worse, pressed charges.

"Just remind me never to mess with you in a dark alley," he said jokingly.
His smile was a bit more relaxed now, but Catherine felt at ease knowing that he could be approached so easily about this. After all, she had essentially knocked her boss on his ass at work, and she was certain that she'd lose her job. She brought her hands up to her cheeks as her eyes began to tear up slightly.

"And if there is anything you need," he said.

"You let me know, okay?"
Catherine nodded her head.

"Thank you," she said, with a slightly choking voice.

"Actually, there is one thing. When can I come back to work? I've missed everyone a lot more than I expected."

"When you're ready," replied Dr. Warner. "You come and see me, and I'll take care of everything. However, I've been asked by the college to hold off on the issue of tenure for a while – just until you're completely recovered, then we can approach it again."

"I understand," Catherine replied. She thanked him again for his time and understanding, apologizing once again for his wounds. He nodded toward her with a kind smile as she left his office, feeling that the weight of the world had been lifted from her shoulders. But, as she walked out the door, Dr. Warner glanced back up at her with a look of grave concern.

Now, she made her way to her own office, where a banner had been taped across the door that said 'Welcome Back, Dr. Thomaston!' She carefully pulled the tape off and rolled up the banner, as she planned on saving it as a memento of her return. Upon opening her office door, she was suddenly faced with the ghost of that day when her life collapsed down around her ankles. She noticed her keys still on her desk and, picking them up, she found that they seemed especially clean. The thought that Nancy had probably cleaned them of any dried blood had crossed her mind. Catherine slowly sat in her chair and looked around at her desk. Her books and notes had been carefully rearranged and organized on her desk. Thank God for teaching assistants. She closed the door halfway and continued to sit in silence. There were no more voices, no shadows lurking in the hall outside her door. She would still discover that under moments of stress, she would hallucinate the smell of smoke. This happened on two occasions during her treatment at AMHI. She knew it wasn't real, but the experience terrified her nonetheless. Moments later, Nancy stuck her head in the door.

"Hey, how's it going?" she asked. "Dr. Warner said you were in the building, so I thought I'd stop by."

Nancy stepped in and sat down in a chair across from her.

"So, when do you think you'll be back in front of a classroom?" Nancy asked. "Not that there's any hurry. It'd just be nice to see you get back in the saddle. And, not to pressure you, but your students miss you."

This led Catherine to believe that she still had a future at Bowdoin and after everything she'd been through, the college once again felt like home.

Upon entering the classroom for the first time since her discharge, her students stood and applauded her return. Everyone knew that Catherine had been very ill, but very few knew why or the fact that she had attacked the head of the department. She once again jumped headfirst into what she loved most – teaching. But it wasn't long until she realized that the ongoing treatment was affecting her abilities. She was unable to focus on the concepts she was trying to convey, and her short-term memory began to suffer. Catherine started referring to her notes more often and would occasionally be caught repeating herself. More disturbingly, she saw her verbal skills changing. Before her illness, she had an ironclad command of the English language. Now, she displayed a noticeable tendency of forgetting a few of the most basic elements of usage, leaving her speech to become somewhat hesitant as she strained to find words for the simplest things. This led Catherine to feel very frustrated, and she began to question her ability to teach. When she wasn't in the classroom, she could almost always be found in her office. Catherine took the time to rearrange it in an attempt to hide from the events that led to her admission to AMHI. She needed to create a comfort zone in her office had become, not just a place to work, but a sanctuary from the frustration she felt in the classroom.

This became a topic of several conversations between Catherine and Nancy, mostly taking place in her office.

"Well, can't you lower your meds a little?" Nancy asked.

"Are you kidding?" Catherine replied. "I'm holding on by my fingernails as it is, and every once in a while, I catch the smell of smoke. The doctors at AMHI said it's part of my illness that I'm going to have to adjust to."

"Oh, my God," said Nancy. "Why didn't you tell me this? This could be a big deal."

"I know," Catherine replied. "I guess I thought that everything would just go back to normal. I just want to move on with my life."

"I know," said Nancy. "But the doctors said that this was chronic. You're going to have to find a way to deal with this every day of your life. I know that sounds impossible and even a bit harsh, but sweetie, that's just the way it is."
Catherine began to feel a bit sick at heart over the realization that she would, essentially, be sick for the rest of her life. That weekend, she went to Farmington to spend some long overdue time with her mother. This would be the first time she'd seen her since her father died, and Catherine arrived prepared to spend a few days with her. Her mother met her on the front walk.

"Catherine!" she said. "How are you?"
Her mother walked up and put both arms around her waist, hugging her with all the strength her frail body could muster. She led Catherine in by the hand and insisted that she have some tea. Her mother then cut to the chase.

"How are you feeling?" she asked, while gently taking her hand.

"Nancy kept me up on your treatment when you were in the hospital. That must have been so terrifying. You know I would have been there for you, but…"

"Mom," Catherine replied. "It's okay. They didn't want me to have visitors anyway."
Her mother nodded her head, but Catherine still sensed her mother's regret of not being there for her when she was at the lowest point of her life. Her mother returned to the kitchen table with two mugs of hot tea. She set them on the table and began to speak a bit hesitantly.

"Catherine," she started. "A long time ago, your father started a trust for you -- just a little rainy day fund. He saw such promise in you and, well, your brother… he was just never on at all. We never could figure him out. But, your father left something for you."
 She got up from her chair and retrieved the envelope.

"I asked them to send the current value of the account and I haven't opened it. I thought you should be the one to do that."
She handed Catherine the envelope, which bore the return address of a local bank. "I know it's not much," her mother said. "But, nowadays, anything helps." Catherine opened the envelope and scanned over the letter. As she read the letter, her eyes slowly widened with shock.

"Holy Shit!" she exclaimed. "Mom, this is seven million dollars!"

Her mother began giggling.

"Yes, I know," she said. "But you should see your face!"

"But, Mom," Catherine replied, still in a state of shock. "I have a job, and you need this more than I do."

"Catherine," her mother said. "Your father left me with more than I'll ever need and considering what you've been through, you may someday be unable to work. But, your father set this up for your retirement, so you wouldn't have to struggle."

"Mom," Catherine replied. "My job is fine."

"And what about tenure?" her mother asked. After Catherine's father had been the president of Farmington College long enough, her mother had picked up on how the system works.

"Well," Catherine replied. "The college has decided to hold off on that for a while."
Her mother raised an eyebrow and gave Catherine that 'I told you so' look. She tried to be convincing, telling her mother that things would be okay. But deep down, she began to feel a faint gnawing that told her that her mother might be right. They spent the weekend talking, as mother and daughter and as friends. They seemed to spend a considerable amount of time talking about William -- both the husband and the father. Sunday afternoon came far too soon and, Catherine found herself on the road, headed back to Bowdoin after giving her mother a much-

needed hug and a kiss on the cheek. And after an uneventful two-hour drive, she pulled into her driveway, carried her bags into her house, and collapsed on the couch. She missed her mother already and reached the unfortunate conclusion that considering her brother's attitude, her mother was all she had left. This was a difficult idea for her to grasp, but she tried not to think about it. Catherine returned to the classroom on Monday, feeling recharged, and made a surprise visit to Nancy's office.

"Hey, girl!" Catherine said from the doorway.

"Hey, Cath," Nancy replied. "How's your mom doing?"

"She's actually doing pretty well," Catherine said, somewhat hesitantly.

"Alright, come on in," said Nancy. Catherine sat down next to her desk as Nancy got up and closed the door.

"Okay, spill it. What's going on?" They were such close friends, that they almost seemed to know what the other was thinking. Catherine sat back into the chair, sliding down into a relaxed position, and sighed with concern.

"I'm starting to wonder about my ability to teach," she said. Nancy looked at her with both surprise and deep concern.

"Cath," she said. "You love to teach! Teaching is your life! What the hell else would you do?"

"I haven't gotten that far yet," Catherine answered. "My mom seems to have this idea that my teaching days may be numbered by my illness, and her instincts have always been right."

"Yeah," Nancy replied. "Doesn't that just piss you off? How did they do that, anyway?"
After a brief pause, Catherine added,

"I'm starting to think she might be right."

"Look," Nancy said, rather sternly. "Sure, your mom may have a point, but you have to think this through yourself. It's your career, and it's your life."

"I know," said Catherine. "I just want all this to go away. Why the fuck can't I just go back to the way it used to be?!"

"I wish I had an answer for you," Nancy replied.

A few weeks later, Catherine was notified that she'd been selected to serve on the college's doctoral committee. She was now one of a handful of professors in the physics department who would read the dissertations of doctoral candidates to question them on the soundness of their ideas and research. In effect, challenging their work and acting as part of a key approval process in the awarding of Ph.D.'s. And while Catherine felt honored to be chosen for the committee, she also realized that meant more responsibility and therefore more stress. But, she also thought it would be a good career move and maybe make her more valuable to the department.

It was now finals week, and they were exams to give, papers to read, and grades to post. Every professor felt the stress of finals week. But for Catherine, this became magnified by her illness and she still had difficulty concentrating, which only made matters worse. She began losing sleep and started to become irritable. The people working in her department now noticed a change in her demeanor, and most simply thought it was the stress of finals week. After all, every professor – even the teaching assistants – felt the stress. But, Catherine was not handling it well at all. In fact, she was just barely holding on to her sanity. Then, during the last exam of the semester, everything unraveled.

In the middle of the exam, Catherine felt her heart begin to race as she detected the strong smell of smoke in the room. She thought it was just stress, but when the smell made her cough, she cleared the classroom for fear of an electrical fire and pulled the alarm. The fire department rushed to the college and upon entering the classroom they began a careful search for any signs of a fire. They found nothing and by the time the students were allowed back into the room, forty-five minutes had passed and many were not able to finish the exam. So it was decided that it would be graded on a curve, based on the questions that each student had already answered.

At the end of the exam, Catherine ran to her office. She could no longer hide from what the stress of her job was doing to her. She threw open her office door and went to sit in her chair when she discovered her legs would no longer work. She began hyperventilating as her muscles progressively tightened, leaving her unable to walk. Catherine braced herself as she fell to the floor, shaking uncontrollably. The department secretary heard what she thought was the sound of someone falling and began searching nearby offices. It didn't take long to find Catherine lying on the floor of her office. The secretary immediately called an ambulance, fearing that Catherine may be having a seizure or worse.

By the time the ambulance arrived, the episode had largely passed. But it was insisted that Catherine go to the hospital for evaluation. And after spending about twenty minutes with the emergency room's attending physician, it was strongly suspected that she'd experienced a panic attack. And upon discharge, she was told to go home, take one milligram of Lorazepam and get some sleep. She began to fearfully anticipate that if an ambulance ever came for her again, she would find herself back within the familiar white walls of AMHI. This frightened her almost as much as the thought that she might someday lose her mind forever, and it was this terrifying possibility that would, on some level, always be with her – never releasing her from its grip.

However, when Catherine got home, the first thing she did was to call Nancy, who arrived about twenty minutes later. Catherine was still visibly shaken by what she had experienced and felt that it was time for some soul-searching.

"I thought I was dying," she told Nancy, with tears coming to her eyes. "I can't do this anymore. It's too hard!"

Nancy could only sit and listen while holding her hand and watch as Catherine's life, once again, began to fall apart.

"I don't think I can go back," she said. "This is such bullshit! I can't do this anymore!"

"Cath," Nancy said. "We'll find a way. There has to be an answer."

She was trying to be reassuring, but Nancy knew that Catherine was right and this was very likely the end of her career. She breathed a heavy sigh of frustration.

"Okay," she said. "Let's just say that you made the decision to resign. Then what? How are you going to make a living? What are you going to do?"

Catherine had not yet told her about the trust her father had left her, as her intention was to use it for retirement.

"Well, actually," she started, with a grin. "I was at my mom's house for a couple of days recently, and she gave me a letter from a local bank."

"Yeah…" Nancy said inquisitively.

"It seems that my father set up a trust for me when I was a kid," Catherine said, rather hesitantly. "I was going to use it for retirement, but when this shit started, I thought that maybe, if I was forced to retire early…"

"Okay," Nancy interrupted. "How much are we talking about, a couple hundred thousand? That's petty cash these days, and it's not going to get you through retirement, is it?"
Catherine looked at Nancy a bit teasingly and momentarily bit at the side of her lip.

"Um … actually," she began. "The value of the trust is seven million dollars."
Nancy sat with her elbows on the table and her hands on the sides of her head. Her mouth had fallen open in sheer disbelief at what she had just heard.

"You're fucking kidding me," she said in a state of shock. "Your father left you seven million dollars, and you're worried about keeping your job?! Seriously?"
Catherine glanced down at the table.

"The plan was to save it until retirement and I love teaching so much," she replied. "But it doesn't look like things have worked out the way I'd hoped. I don't know, maybe it's time. With the way things have been going, it kind of seems like I'm not much of a teacher anymore."

"Don't you think you're being a bit too hard on yourself?" Nancy asked. "You could still do research and get published. You can still make your mark."

"Yeah, I could do that," said Catherine thoughtfully. "But I still need the college to back up my research."

"Mmm… maybe," Nancy wondered aloud. "Maybe the college would be willing to keep you on as an unpaid adjunct. That way, you can still contribute to the sciences and be involved with the college, to some degree. You could still feel a sense of purpose, Cath."

"It's definitely worth looking into," Catherine agreed. "But, I need to take this one step at a time."

The next day, Catherine composed her letter of resignation to Dr. Warner. Even as she typed it up, she still found it unbelievable that she was about to leave a job she had centered her life around. Teaching physics was all she knew as she sat in front of her PC, wondering what the next step would be. She thought about the possibility of staying with her mother for a while, just until her trust fund started to pay out. But, it didn't take much time for Catherine to decide that she didn't want to burden her mother and that it might be a better idea to simply move a bit closer to her instead. Nancy had already offered to take her in for as long as it took for her to begin receiving her trust fund, but Catherine told her that she'd think about it while she considered all of her options. After the letter printed out, Catherine decided to leave it on her desk at home for a couple of days. She felt that it was important to absorb what she was about to do before she did it. The following day, she called the bank that was administering her trust fund. She was told that the funds would be released in monthly payments when she turned forty.

"You don't understand," she said. "I can't work anymore because I have a mental illness." She paused for a moment on the phone to let those words sink in. Catherine had never actually thought of herself as being mentally ill until she heard she heard herself say it. The woman on the phone told her that the only way to get access to the account was to have a judge sign off on a statement of disability. She would also have to provide records that demonstrated the severity of her illness, as well as a statement from her psychiatrist. The statement wouldn't be a problem, and she could file a 'request of information' with AMHI for her inpatient records. She would later keep these documents so that she could study them further.

Now, Catherine needed the paperwork for a statement of disability, and she knew that the

County Clerk's office would probably have what she needed. So she called their office and had them forward the correct forms to her. She explained her situation to her psychiatrist at her next visit, as well as the decision she made to leave her job. Dr. Beach understood her reasons and had the statement produced by his office. Upon meeting with her attorney, he told Catherine that he would present all the records she gathered to a judge as the larger part of her case. An appointment was made and Catherine's attorney accompanied her as she stood before the judge to argue her case. And it didn't take long for the judge to see that Catherine was in a very unfortunate situation, and freed up the funds that she so desperately needed. She would not receive a lump sum but, instead, Catherine was to receive a monthly stipend of five thousand dollars. This would be enough money to pay all her bills, mortgage, car payments, and insurance, as well as the necessities of life. The next day, she delivered her letter of resignation to Dr. Warner's office.

Catherine walked into his office without an appointment and knocked on the door.

"Please, come in and have a seat," he said. He seemed glad to see her and motioned to the chair in front of his desk.

"So, how are you?" Dr. Warner asked.

"Well, I'm doing okay," Catherine replied. "I wanted to apologize for what happened during finals week. I guess I was having a bad day."

"Catherine," he replied reassuringly. "The important thing is that you're okay. Besides, everything worked out."

After a few moment's pause, Catherine handed him an envelope.

"There is something else I wanted to talk to you about," she said.

Dr. Warner took the envelope and skimmed over the letter.

"You're leaving us?" he asked, looking up at her quizzically.

"Things just aren't working anymore," she said. "My illness has affected my ability to teach. I can't be around people anymore because I get this feeling like everyone's constantly judging me and when I get stressed, I start to smell smoke. I just don't think I can do this anymore, and the department needs a reliable teacher."

Dr. Warner let out a sigh of resolve.

"Well," he started. "You've obviously put a great deal of thought into your decision and having seen some of the things you've gone through, I can't say I'm completely surprised. But, I have to say that I've developed a considerable degree of respect for you. In your place, I'm not sure how I'd handle it. You must be a very strong person."

"Sometimes, I'm not so sure," Catherine replied.

She had become somewhat uncomfortable and wanted nothing more than to leave. "I know that my resignation says two weeks, but I like to leave before the semester starts."

"That sounds like a good idea," Dr. Warner said. "Tell you what. If you want today to be your last day, that's fine with me. I'll make sure you get paid for the full two weeks. Sound okay?"

"Thank you very much," Catherine replied. She stood up from the chair rather awkwardly, and Dr. Warner stood up as well.

"Good luck, Catherine," he said. "And if there's anything you need, just pick up the phone."

"I'll keep that in mind," she said. "Thank you again."

She did her best to control her emotions, but her eyes began to tear up even before she left his office. Walking quickly out of the building, Catherine sat in her car and began crying. She felt a twinge of doubt as to what she'd just done, but she also knew that it was for the best. She made a short drive home to get some rest, as well as to give some thought about what the next step should be. After all, teaching was her life and she would always miss it. During her previous soul-searching, she thought maybe at some point, she could become a tutor. Not for the money, but for the joy of teaching. But that was a decision for another time, and she needed to prioritize. Fifteen minutes later, Nancy knocked on her door. She had called Catherine earlier but only got her answering machine. So, feeling a bit uneasy, she decided to go over to Catherine's place just to make sure everything was okay.

"Come on in," Catherine yelled. Nancy opened the door and walked in.

"Things okay?" she asked.

"Uh… yeah," replied Catherine. "I turned in my resignation today. I guess I would have done it sooner, but I had to deal with my trust first."

"That's a good idea," Nancy said. "You want to make sure you're not going to end up in the poor house."
Catherine nodded her head in agreement and then became noticeably quiet.

"You want to talk about it?" Nancy asked.

"I'm not sure there's anything to talk about," replied Catherine. "I've already had a good cry about it. But now, I feel like it's over. I almost feel relieved."

"That's great, Cath!" Nancy said. "I was really worried about you, and I wasn't sure how you'd handle resigning from your job. So how did Dr. Warner handle it?"  "He wasn't completely surprised. But, he now thinks of me as a stronger person," Catherine replied.

"So, what's next?" Nancy asked.

"Well," Catherine said with a slight smirk.

"You want to go house hunting?"
Nancy became visibly excited over this.

"Hell, yeah!" She exclaimed. "I love house hunting! Where were you thinking of going?"

"Some place isolated, but closer to my mom," Catherine answered.

"You know, just in case something happens."

"Have you talked to your doctor lately, just to bring him up to speed on everything?" Nancy asked.

"I have an appointment tomorrow," Catherine said. "He'll get the full story then."

"Okay," said Nancy. "Hey, I'll go get some newspapers, and we can start looking at houses. And let's order some pizza."

"Sounds good," said Catherine.
They were up late into the night, eating pizza and looking at the real estate pages of every newspaper Nancy could find.

"How about a colonial?" Nancy asked. "You know something dignified."

"Sounds expensive," replied Catherine. "Besides, I'm looking for something a bit rustic – something down-to-earth."

"I hear you," said Nancy. "Oh, look at this one. This is a log cabin in the Carrabassett Valley, just north of Farmington. It's near the edge of Stratton Pond, right below the south face of Mount Bigelow. Cath, it's perfect. It's fairly close to your mom, and it's in a fantastic location!"

"Sounds great!" Catherine replied. "But how much?"
Nancy pointed to the article.

"That's not bad," she said.

"Oh, I don't know," replied Catherine. "It's half a million dollars."

"Cath," Nancy started. "You have seven million dollars, and you don't have to pay for the house outright. So, you make mortgage payments like anyone else – big deal. This looks like a really nice place!"

Catherine paused a bit to compose her thoughts.

"I need to see it before I make an offer," Catherine said.

"I would love to see this place," Nancy replied. "Hey! It'll be a road trip!"

Catherine looked over at her.

"A road trip it is!" Catherine said.

They turned and high-fived each other and made plans to call the number on the listing for an appointment. But, in spite of the choice that was made, they continued looking through the real estate listings. However, it seemed that there was nothing else that was remotely comparable to a cabin near a pond in the mountains. She got on the web, looking at the real estate market for the entire state of Maine. But somehow, she always found herself going back to the cabin that Nancy found in the newspaper. She investigated it more thoroughly and began making some phone calls. Catherine didn't dare handle all of this on her own, so she hired a real estate agent. An appointment was made to go up and look at the property, and Nancy quickly volunteered to go

along. So, they made the four-hour drive to
Carrabassett Valley and upon seeing the cabin,
Catherine immediately fell in love with it.

"You have to make an offer," said Nancy.
"Don't let this one get away. You'll be closer to
your mom but still have your space, and this place
is gorgeous."

Upon talking to the real estate agent,
Catherine was told that because of the location,
the asking price had gone up a bit. But, she
wanted it enough that she made an offer anyway.
Over the next week, the only other offer had been
withdrawn. A contract was signed, and now it was
only a matter of time. Catherine spent that time
packing and making other arrangements. Again,
burying herself in the process. She wouldn't have
to think about what she feared the most if she
could lose herself in the complexities of
purchasing a home. During the month and a half
before closing, Catherine involved herself in
every aspect of the process – from the inspection
to some basic home repairs. She spent several
nights there, and Nancy thought it might be a
good idea to go up with her. After all, Catherine
would, essentially, be living in the middle of
nowhere and Nancy wanted to be sure she could
acclimate to living in such isolation. But, in spite
of her concerns, Catherine seemed to be in her
glory. She had purchased her first home in a

location that seemed fit for the setting of a storybook.

"Imagine what this place will look like in the fall," Catherine said excitedly.

It had been a long time since she felt this good, and it now seemed that she was on a mission to start her life over again. Hopefully, Nancy thought, there was indeed such a thing as second chances.

A week before the closing, Catherine began planning for the move. She thought about hiring a moving company but wanted to save some money, and she thought that doing it herself might be something of an adventure. But, when the day came, Catherine looked around her apartment and realized just how much there was to move. So, she decided it would be a good idea to rent a truck and wasted no time picking up the phone and calling the nearest rental company. Her next call was to Nancy. Catherine needed to update her on the moving van. It would be a lot easier to simply pack up one moving van, instead of making multiple car trips, and who knows how long that would take.

Chapter 5

The move went flawlessly and with Nancy's help, Catherine was able to remain focused and organized. It was June, and Nancy decided to spend the week with Catherine at her new home. She felt that suddenly leaving Catherine in such isolation might cause her to slip into a relapse. Then, around the middle of the week, Nancy stepped out for a few hours, leaving Catherine a note on her coffee table that read simply, 'Be back later, Nancy.' A few hours later, she returned with a small animal carrier.

"I'm back!" Nancy called out. "And I brought a friend!"
Catherine was cleaning the bathroom when she heard Nancy's voice. She got up and walked into the living room, her curiosity aroused by Nancy's words.

"What do you mean, a friend?" Catherine asked. Nancy quickly opened the carrier and gently took out a nine-month-old kitten.

"See, I brought a friend!" she said.

"Oh, my God!" Catherine said excitedly. "She's so cute!"

"Actually," replied Nancy. "She's a he. I thought you might like having a man around the house."
She handed Catherine the small gray bundle of fur, who gently held the kitten to her chest. Nancy

had also purchased all the things that were needed for the raising of the kitten – food, bowls, cat toys, and of course, a box of litter.

"Look at his eyes. They are so beautiful!" Catherine exclaimed.

She walked over to her couch and, after sitting down, began cradling the kitten as if it were an infant. Her eyes welled up with joy as she started speaking to it in baby talk. And with that single interaction, a deep bond had been created – one that could never be broken.

"So, what do we call you?" Catherine asked as the kitten began a series of high-pitched cries.

Nancy sat down on the couch, just far enough away to be able to take in the entire maternal picture.

"He's a Russian Blue," Nancy said.

Catherine held the kitten a few inches away from herself and looked into its deep, golden eyes. It looked back at her with its rounded face and a faint mew.

"Ivan," she declared. "I'm going to call you, Ivan."

She turned toward Nancy and, bringing Ivan to her chest, again smiled broadly. This was something Catherine had not done in months and for Nancy, it meant far more than any words could express.

"Thank you so much!" Catherine said joyfully.

She hugged Nancy around the neck, further expressing her gratitude and excitement.

Nancy thought how good it was to see her being excited, even elated over something – anything. But, she had another reason for giving Catherine the kitten. Nancy knew that she would not always be able to rush to her house at a moment's notice, especially after the fall semester started. Now, she'd know that Catherine would never be truly alone and that caring for another life, no matter how small, might give her a reason to get up every morning. But there was something going on that Nancy was unaware of, something Catherine had not told her about. Catherine had kept herself so involved in the process of purchasing her new home that she had become distracted from her growing fear of going back to AMHI. But now, that fear had begun to manifest itself in a way she found very disturbing – nightmares. Catherine experienced them every night – sometimes twice a night. It was always the same, down to the last detail.

The fall semester began, and Bowdoin College sprang to life with activity. Nancy was unable to visit Catherine due to her teaching schedule but called two or three times a week to make sure things were okay. Meanwhile, Catherine and Ivan were getting along famously. He made it a habit of curling up on her pillow at night and sleeping near her head and as he got larger, he moved down to her hip. His presence seemed to help Catherine relax but did nothing to keep her nightmares at bay. She continued to go to weekly sessions with Dr. Beach, but told him Catherine's new feline friend and believed that Ivan would be very therapeutic for her, hoping that this just might keep her from relapsing.

Winter in the Carrabassett Valley arrived early and struck with a vengeance second only to the anger of the gods. Catherine listened to the weather and traffic reports often on her radio. After all, she was living out in the middle of nowhere. And regardless of the kind of day she might be having, Ivan was always nearby, bringing her a degree of comfort she hadn't known since before her father died. Due to her illness, Catherine had begun to experience the winter blues and started sleeping late into the morning. But mading his wishes known that it was time for breakfast, Ivan would paw at her face and cry loudly. When this came to the attention of Dr. Beach, he raised her dose of Lexapro. She had been on this antidepressant since her treatment at AMHI and the doctor adjusted it to help her combat what he referred to as 'Seasonal Affective Disorder'. Catherine would continue on this new dose indefinitely.

It was during the winter break that Nancy finally was able to visit after the roads had been cleared of what the first nor'easter left behind. She stayed for about a week, partly to get away from the stress of work, but mostly to see how Catherine was doing. She hoped that Ivan's presence was having a positive impact on Catherine's mood as well as her of mind. Before the week was out, Nancy was convinced that Catherine was keeping her head well above water. She was even fairly convinced that Ivan's presence was having a positive effect, in that Catherine seemed more herself. But, Nancy still didn't know about Catherine's nightmares and Catherine would continue to hide this from her, fearing that Nancy might become concerned for her sanity.

Nancy left at week's end to return for the spring semester, feeling confident that Catherine's life may be taking on a positive direction. Winter has finally passed and spring began with a few showers and small storms, but mostly a lot of rain. In Maine, spring was commonly referred to as 'mud season' and near the mountains, the spring runoff made things that much worse. It flooded roads, created sinkholes in the highway, and in general made the lives of everyone in the valley miserable. But through mud, flooding, and patience, summer finally arrived. But, even after all this time, living in her new house for about a year as well as Ivan's comforting presence, her nightmares, which only continued, became more intense. And to make matters worse, she began to feel as if she was being watched. It wasn't something that she found to be especially stressful, just a twinge that quietly gnawed away at her. She tried to blow it off as the result of living in such an isolated area, and that maybe it was the silence of the woods playing tricks on her. However, it was enough to occasionally frighten her when it occurred suddenly and only served to reinforce her deep fears of returning to AMHI.

At this point, she decided, once again, that she needed a distraction – something she could involve herself in as completely as possible. She went outside to clear her head and upon looking at the grandness of the Bigelow Range, she was struck with the idea of taking up hiking. It should have been obvious to her, but her thinking had become muddied by the nightly torments she'd been experiencing. Catherine thought back to her one and only hike, for which she was entirely unprepared, but this time things would be different. She knew that Nancy had been hiking for years and thought it might be best to learn from someone with experience.  Walking quickly back to the cabin, she excitedly called Nancy, but would never mention the nightmares or the strange feelings she was having. She didn't want Nancy to worry about her and wanted to give her the impression that things were finally settling down.

When Catherine expressed an interest in hiking, Nancy saw it not only as something of a breakthrough for her but also the chance to acquire a hiking buddy. They got together almost every weekend, going over Nancy's hiking books and topographical maps. Nancy gave her a crash course in the equipment she'd need and tips on first aid, survival, and wilderness skills. Catherine soaked it up like a sponge and looked forward to their first hike with great anticipation. They set their sights on the first week of October, at the peak of autumn. This would be a perfect first hike for Catherine, as the temperature wouldn't be warm enough to induce heat stroke nor cool enough to worry about hypothermia. She chose Little Bigelow as their first hike. After ending up in the hospital last summer, she felt compelled to conquer it. Nancy arrived early on a Saturday morning with water bottles, a guidebook, and some energy bars, as well as the usual equipment she carried when she went hiking. The weather was perfect for a day hike and Catherine was well-prepared. The sky was a deep, beautiful blue and the temperature was about seventy-two degrees. As Catherine was still an inexperienced hiker, Nancy made sure to keep the pace light, and they started out on the trail near Stratton Pond, just outside Catherine's doorstep. After about two miles, Little Bigelow came rising into view. It stood as the first of a rocky row of peaks against a cloudless sky of royal blue. The colors of autumn lit up like a wildfire as far as the eye could see. Another twenty minutes went by before they started the climb up its rocky slope, stopping every once in a while for rest and water. The hike up the slope was difficult, but Catherine had been doing a lot of jogging and stuck to the training program that the two of them had put together. Finally, they got to the top. The view was magnificent, with fall colors flowing like an ocean down into the valley and the remaining peaks of the Bigelow range vaulting high above their heads. For Nancy, this was a short hike. She was used to much more difficult places like the knife edge at Katahdin and Mount Washington. But for Catherine, this was a conquest, not simply a victory over a relatively small mountain peak, but an achievement that seemed to overshadow a life filled with mental anguish and pain. She stood on the very top of the rocky summit with arms outstretched, yelling in celebration as though challenging the gods themselves. After another thirty minutes, they started back down the mountain. It took far less time to get back, but Catherine also discovered new muscles that she rarely used until now.

<h1 style="text-align:center">Chapter 7</h1>

Nancy visited as often as her schedule would allow. Sometimes they'd go on a small hike and other times just to sit and talk. She scolded Catherine fiercely upon discovering that she had taken up smoking."Are you fucking nuts?! Do you know what that shit can do to you?!" Nancy asked with both shock and disbelief.
Catherine shrugged her shoulders a bit.

"It calms my nerves," she replied, sounding as though she was trying to convince herself more than Nancy.

"So, what's going on?" Nancy said. She was concerned that her friend might be falling apart again.

"The psych visits are getting a little more complicated."
Catherine tried to be vague.

"What do you mean, complicated?" Nancy inquired.

"Well, for a long time, my sessions have been nothing more than things like where I am on the mood scale, how I'm feeling, and medication side effects. Things have been simple. But now, it just seems like the questions are getting more complicated. My psychiatrist has been asking about things like hearing voices and smelling smoke. And he's started asking questions about my past and my parents. Shit! I got sick in my early thirties. What does my past have to do with anything?" Catherine complained.

"Maybe he sees something that you're not picking up on. Have you asked him about it?" Nancy asked.

"I'm not sure I want to. I guess I'm afraid of what he might say. And I'm not fucking going back to AMHI!" Catherine said in an agitated voice.

"You don't know that that's going to happen." Nancy tried to be reassuring.

"I know, but I'm scared." Catherine's voice began to quiver a bit.

"So when is your next appointment?" Nancy asked.

"Tomorrow," Catherine answered.

"Promise me you'll ask," Nancy pleaded. Catherine nodded her head, trying unsuccessfully to hold back a torrent of tears while crossing her arms into her stomach and rocking back and forth slightly. Nancy stayed with her for another twenty minutes, holding her hand and trying to be reassuring. But secretly, Nancy had some serious doubts about Catherine's state of mind, as well as the direction of her treatment.

## Chapter 8

The next morning, Catherine decided on a morning hike around Stratton Pond and stopped at its far side, sitting on a large rock to rest. She looked up at the Bigelow range and remembered her hike to the top with Nancy. Now, the August heat had shrouded the mountains in an almost opaque veil of haze. She sat on the rock watching the water rippling near her feet, wondering what the outcome of her psych appointment would be. Nancy's attempt to comfort her yesterday didn't do much to calm the terrifying possibility of going back to AMHI. She started back, continuing around Stratton Pond until she returned home. Upon entering her front door, Catherine unclipped the belt that her water bottle hung from and tossed it on the couch. She sat in the chair nearest her father's picture and looked into his eyes. "Daddy, I don't want to go," she muttered to herself more than to the image of her father.

The tears welled up again, and she pulled her knees up into the fetal position, with her arms wrapped around her knees. She began to cry softly to herself, tucking her face into her knees as though she was trying to hide and drifted off into a light sleep. She woke with a start from the half-hour chime of the clock on the wall. Catherine noticed that it was two thirty and her appointment was at four o'clock. It would take an hour to get to Franklin Memorial's medical arts building, so she had to get ready a little faster than usual.

Catherine left for her psychiatrist's appointment. She scratched Ivan on the top of the head as she left, and he tipped his head up, closing his eyes. He loved having his head scratched and purred loudly as he pushed toward Catherine's fingertips. Catherine left the cabin, closing the door firmly behind her and making sure it was locked. Walking over to her car, she opened it remotely and climbed in. She drove a Nissan 350 Z, having had it special ordered in forest green, she considered it to be the perfect fusion of practicality, efficiency, and speed. With a noticeable touch of the sexy sports car she'd always dreamed of having. The interior was jet black with gun metal gray trim, and the seats were covered with black leather. At night, the arch-shaped dash lit up with a multitude of indicators and lighted buttons, with a heads-up display of the speedometer reflecting off the lower left windshield. Catherine often thought that this must be what it was like to sit in the cockpit of an F-27, and driving it at night gave her a bit of a rush. Whenever she gunned the engine, Catherine would swear it sounded like the brief roar of a lion. She crept slowly down the dirt road that led to Route 27 and as she pulled out into the southbound lane, the car's tires kicked out a bit of loose dirt from the road. Catherine tried to be careful how she pulled out into traffic, but secretly she loved the sound the tires made as they spit out the dry, loose dirt and gravel.

As she began the drive to Farmington, Catherine began to unconsciously grip the wheel tightly enough to whiten her knuckles. She'd release her grip and then tighten it back up again. She caught herself doing it when one of her knuckles cracked. Catherine was very well aware of the reason for her anxiety. Ten miles into her drive, she glanced at the heads-up display.

"Holy shit," she muttered, with both surprise and disbelief.

The speedometer read 72 miles an hour. Now, it occurred to her that she had to relax and slow down. After all, she reasoned to herself, this could all be in her imagination. Sometimes, Catherine would get an idea in her head and get herself worked up over it. Then later, as events unfolded, she'd realize that her anxiety was caused only by herself. She began driving east, past Sugarloaf Mountain. The trails were bare and empty, but the mountain didn't need snow for its beauty to be seen. She started the turn south and within 5 or 10 minutes the peak of Mount Abraham began to show itself through the thin summer haze. Catherine always found the mountains both glorious and incredibly soothing. At home, she would spend hours lying on a large flat rock on the far side of Stratton Pond, where she'd gaze up at the Bigelow range and ponder her own smallness in the shadow of its earthly beauty. This, of course, led her thoughts off into the rest of the universe. She was always fascinated by the insignificance of the human race. But, she was even more fascinated by the number of people who didn't seem to understand or care about it. "So much more." she would think to herself.

She continued driving down Route 27 when she realized something was missing – music. Catherine pulled over slightly and slowed down as she reached over for her CD case. She opened it and slipped out the first disc in the case. Sliding the disc into her car's CD player, she pushed a couple of buttons skipping a few tracks, and suddenly Catherine was surrounded with music. It was her favorite band, Rush. She had skipped ahead to her favorite song from their 'Moving Pictures' CD, called 'Red Barchetta'. She considered the tune to be the perfect driving music, and the drum rhythms created a kind of energy that made her feel alive. Soon, Catherine was singing along. She belted out the lyrics like a rock star while rocking her head forward and back in time to the music.

Catherine continued driving south on Route 27 and listening to the rest of the CD, she noticed

Blue Mountain coming up on her right. She glanced up at its summit thinking about what a wonderful hike it would be and immediately thought about Nancy, that she should call her when she returned home. Maybe she'd be interested in planning a hike there this fall. Catherine pulled off to the side of the road and turned on her flashers. Looked at her watch, she wondered if there might have a few minutes to get out and just stand there, looking at the mountain.

"Just a few minutes," she thought. She wondered how many trails went to the summit and which were the safest. If she could conquer Blue Mountain, it would be the high point of her life. And she would quickly come to realize that she could do anything she set her mind to. "This time, Blue Mountain – next time, mental illness", she quietly said to herself. Catherine had developed a determination to do this, and she now felt the passion she needed to succeed. She got back in her car and proceeded down Route 27 until she passed a sign that said, 'Now Entering Farmington'. The tension and anxiety began to return, as the sign now reminded her of why she was on the road in the first place. Catherine's knuckles whitened up again as she began to grip the wheel. This time, she kept a close watch on her speed.

# Chapter 9

She soon found herself in downtown Farmington. It wasn't nearly as busy or as large as Portland and within a few minutes, Catherine was turning right at Route 133 onto Franklin Health Commons and into the parking lot of the hospital. The medical arts building was on the far side of the hospital, and she parked in front of the building, just to the left of the door. Today, Catherine was very much on edge and fearful of the idea that she might be facing a second trip to AMHI.

Her psychiatrist, Dr. Howard Beach, had been overseeing her care from the beginning. She always felt that he seemed to know more about her than she knew about herself, and that made her feel uncomfortable. Dr. Beach had two offices – one in Brunswick and the other in Farmington. Catherine walked into room 108. Walking into the waiting area, she sat in a corner chair. By this point, Catherine had become so uncomfortable around people that she began to slowly gravitate towards isolation. When the secretary called her name, she stepped up to the desk and checked in. A nearby office door opened and Dr. Beach stuck his head out and called Catherine in. Once again, she sat in the leather chair, sliding down into a relaxed position.

"So, how are things?" he asked, looking up from her chart.

"I'm doing pretty well."
She tried to sound convincing, thinking that if she believed her own words, then he might too.

"I hear a bit of discomfort in your voice. What's going on?" he inquired.

"Shit!" she thought to herself. "Why does he have to be so fucking perceptive?" So, she brought him up to date on everything that had happened – the arrival of the fire department, the panic attack, and her resignation from Bowdoin College.

"I can't help but be a bit concerned, Catherine," said Dr. Beach. "How are you going to make a living? I'd rather not see you having any more issues due to lack of funds."
To any therapist, this would be a valid concern. But Catherine had not yet mentioned the trust fund her father left her.

"Well," she began. "My father left me a trust fund, so I'll be living off that plus what I've saved up. I didn't want to resign until the payments started coming in."
 Dr. Beach nodded his head as he wrote in her chart.

"Sounds like you've thought this through," he said.
He nodded his head in the thoughtful way that any other psychiatrist would. Glancing back at her

chart, he began reviewing her medication list with her – drugs, amounts, and dosages.

"Any side effects?" he asked.

Catherine was well aware of the fact that a side effect could present itself at any time, regardless of how long she'd been taking the medication. So she looked up the side effects of all her meds on the internet and kept a watchful eye for signs of trouble, without letting this vigilance rule her life.

"Not really, but some nights I have a hard time getting to sleep," she replied.

He nodded his head again.

"If it becomes a constant occurrence, we can make some changes to the Lorazepam to help you with that," he said.

He paused to scribble a note on his legal pad and asked her where she was on the mood scale. It was the usual list of questions, and Catherine did her best to sound confident.

"Any hallucinations?" he asked.

Catherine became visibly agitated, pulling her knees up into the fetal position. Dr. Beach immediately recognized her anxiety and defensiveness.

"Catherine, what happened?" he asked in a gentle, but concerned voice.

Catherine spoke in a guarded, hesitant manner. "I was just a bit late taking my morning meds – only by a couple of hours," she said.

"Okay. And what happened?" he asked.

"Well," she began, as the doctor gently moved her feet back down to the floor.

"I thought I smelled a bit of smoke in the house," she said cautiously.

"That must be a little scary, considering where you live," he commented.

"You have no idea," she responded.

"And the more it stressed me out, the worse it got."
Now, Catherine realized what she'd said.

"Son of a bitch," she thought, as she silently chastised herself for falling for his probing statement.
She paused momentarily as she tried to find the right words for the question that had been nagging at her for the last few weeks.

"Was there something else?" he asked.
Finally finding her words, Catherine took the risk of getting an answer she might not be comfortable with.

"Considering everything that's happened over the last few weeks, is there any chance that I'll have to go back into the hospital again?"
Dr. Beach looked up from his pad.

"Well, I don't know that it's time to start thinking about that just yet," he said.
His response was very diplomatic, but Catherine was a scientist, and she saw the world through the contrast of black and white.

The doctor's words entered her mind like a forest fire. This was not what she wanted to hear. What she wanted was validation, as if the doctor might completely agree without question. Obviously, that was not going to happen, and she became frightened, seeing her worst fears slowly becoming a reality. Dr. Beach slowly nodded his head once more, while continuing to write on his legal pad.

"Anything else?" he asked.

"That's it," she answered.

"How many times has this happened?" he asked, looking up from his pad and directly into her eyes.

"Just this morning," she replied. The doctor seemed satisfied with Catherine's answer.

She concluded that the doctor's answer wasn't really an answer at all, and his seemingly evasive response only served to bring Catherine's deep fear of returning to AMHI into the harsh light of reality. Up to this point, she had managed to bury this fear – to keep it secret. Now with one brief response, she was forced to confront the possibility of returning to the white, sterile hallways of hell. She nodded confidently, trying desperately to hide the fact that she was terrified beyond words.

"Would an increase in my meds help?" Catherine asked.

"Let's see what we have you on," the doctor replied.

He looked over her medication list, with specific attention to the dosages.

"I don't know if I can increase any of your meds. We can certainly add one if we need to. But I'm thinking it's possible that some of the things you've been experiencing may be situational. That is, maybe, a reaction to stress, and you've been through a lot lately. The last thing I would want is to over-medicate you, because that's no way to live, either. So, let's get you through this transition you're going through first and if there are still some things that need to be ironed out, we'll approach them then."

This seemed like a reasonable plan, despite Catherine's fear of returning to AMHI. Dr. Beach wrote new prescriptions for her meds and concluded their session.

But the fear she had created got the best of her, and now she was emotionally trapped by her own paranoia. She shook his hand and walked out into the parking lot at a rapid pace, with tears in her eyes. Upon getting to her car, she frantically fumbled with her keys, dropping them to the pavement.

"Shit!" she muttered to herself and quickly retrieved them.

After getting into her car and starting the engine, she drove to the other side of the parking lot. She shut off the engine, buried her face in her hands, and began crying uncontrollably.

"What the fuck am I going to do?!" she sobbed. "It's not fair! What the fuck did I do?!" She was almost screaming now, but she was parked well away from the other cars, so no one would see or hear her in her desperate panic.

# Chapter 10

Catherine sat in her car crying for the next 15 minutes when she noticed that her face and hands had become numb, she started the breathing exercise that Dr. Beach taught her. It took another 20 minutes for Catherine to bring herself to the point where she could start her car and begin the drive back home.

On her way, Catherine started to become obsessed with the idea of going back into the hospital. Her logical mind told her that this was an unlikely possibility, but she was slowly becoming more paranoid, and it was gradually beginning to overwhelm her ability to reason clearly. Her response to this was to bury herself in her search for a house. She made her way out of town and just after passing the town's welcome sign, she smelled a bit of smoke in her car. Catherine sniffed at the air and, thinking it might be an engine problem, pulled over and got out.

"Fuck!" she yelled. "I don't have the fucking time for this shit!"
She put her hand on the hood of the car, then took a few steps back – it was only warm. Logic told her there might still be a problem, but instinct whispered in her ear, telling her that she was falling apart. She opened the hood, hoping to find something. That would certainly be better than

losing her mind, and upon examining the engine it was obvious to Catherine that it was in perfect order. She looked closer, still hoping to find a problem. But, there was nothing – no frayed wires, no melted insulation, and all the belts looked like they had just come off the shelf – and she still smelled smoke. She closed the hood, letting it fall into its latch underneath.

"God, this can't be happening!" she said quietly to herself.

She began to think this might be the beginning of something that just might bring her illness out of remission. Stepping back away from her car by about 20 feet, she smelled the air again. This time there was no hint of smoke.

Now, her fear rose out of confusion. She smelled smoke in the car, but there seemed to be nothing wrong, and when she walked away the smell was gone. Catherine went back to the car and knelt by each wheel well in order to feel the brakes.

"Maybe one of them is locking up," she said to herself.

But the car wasn't pulling to one side or another, and the brakes were fairly cool.

"Shit!" she cursed.

She got back in the car and frantically searched for a rational explanation. She felt the dash, checked the ashtray, looked at all the carpets and seats, and found nothing. The smell got stronger, but there was no visible smoke. When Catherine realized this, she knew there was nothing wrong with her car, but there was something wrong and she could feel it. It gnawed at her brain like a single fire ant that somehow found its way into her head, but she didn't want to think about it. She just wanted to get home.

She started her car again and began driving north on Route 27. Her knuckles turned white as she gripped the wheel, and her eyes began to tear up. Catherine's face became flushed as she fought back another bout of tears.

"Oh, God!" she said out loud. "Not now!"
 As soon as she got home, she could take some Lorazepam and get some sleep. Maybe then, this would simply pass, and she could chalk it up as severe anxiety. But, home was about 40 minutes away and Catherine felt as though she was about to fall off the edge of the world, into the dark vacuum of insanity. At the intersection with Route 234, she discovered the highway had been completely blocked by a road crew. They were painting marks on the pavement while setting up a machine that would be used to cut into the asphalt. Catherine pulled over and stopped about 20 feet from the yellow state truck and, still agitated, got out of her car, slammed the door shut, and marched up to the road crew.

"Excuse me, I have to get through," she said.

A broad-shouldered man in an orange vest approached her.

"Sorry, Miss, this part of the road has been closed off. Didn't you see the detour sign back there?" he asked.

"No, I didn't see the detour sign!" she said, rather angrily.

The rest of the road crew stopped working in order to gawk at Catherine as she continued to rant.

"Well, I'm sorry, you're going to have to go back down Route 2 and east to Norridgewock," he instructed.

"I know how to get to fucking Norridgewock!" Catherine yelled impatiently.

"And I don't have that kind of time!"

She was practically begging now. The rest of the road crew occasionally nudged each other and grinned a bit sarcastically, as though silently commenting on Catherine's agitation. One workman leaned over to another and whispered, "What a head case".

She continued pleading with them to let her around.

"I just want to go home," she said.

Her tone was beginning to sound desperate. That's when she noticed the supervisor she'd been yelling at had begun looking her up and down as though she were a side of beef. This made her feel both threatened and angry.

"What the fuck are you looking at?" she demanded.

The supervisor took a step toward her as she clenched both fists in anticipation of a physical confrontation.

"Listen, sweetheart," he said.

His words were gentle and yet felt menacing at the same time.

"Maybe we can… make a deal," he said.

Catherine became visibly uncomfortable and quickly grew to despise all of them.

"That truck over there's pretty big. I'm sure there'd be plenty of room for… all of us," he said. He glanced back at his coworkers and grinned, getting a chuckle from the entire crew.

"I want to know who your boss is, asshole!" she yelled.

The workers who stood behind the supervisor suddenly dropped their tools and stepped forward and formed a line, standing side by side. The supervisor dropped his radio and took a stance exactly as the men lined up behind him.

"What are you doing?" Catherine demanded. "Don't fucking touch me!"

Suddenly, their faces took on a menacing expression, as they began glaring at her with slightly squinted eyes and grinning at her as though with malicious intent.

"Why are you looking at me like that?!" she demanded. "Stop it! I just want to go home!"

The man standing in front of Catherine looked deeply into her eyes.

"What's the matter, Cat? Don't you want to play with us?" he asked.

His voice had become very deep, as though he'd suddenly become possessed. "No… no!"
She began to hyperventilate.

"How do you know my name?!" she demanded.

Catherine went from anger to an overwhelming feeling of terror.

"What the hell is going on?!"

"Come and play with us, Cat. Don't worry, we'll be gentle," he said with a taunting grin. "I promise."

As if on cue, all of them began laughing, making her feel as though she was about to be pulled into some dark, inescapable evil.

Catherine's rant was suddenly interrupted by the sound of a car pulling up.

"Ma'am, can I help you?" a voice asked.
A Maine state police car had stopped just ahead of where she stood.

"Jesus Christ," she exclaimed. "You have no idea how glad I am to see you!"

She sidestepped over to the car, keeping a watchful eye on the men who stood, still glaring at her.

"Look! I just want to get home, and these assholes want me to get into their truck with them! They're acting like they're fucking possessed, and I want them arrested!" she ranted.

"Ma'am, are you okay?" the officer asked.

"Can I call an ambulance for you?"

"Didn't you hear me? I want these assholes arrested!" Her voice was filled with frustration as she pointed back toward the road crew.

"Ma'am… who?" the officer inquired.

Catherine took a deep breath, trying to be patient.

"What do you mean, who?" she asked, as though the officer had been struck dumb. "Them!"

She pointed again, turning back toward the road crew. But there was nothing there – no road crew, no equipment, no lines painted on the pavement. In fact, the dirt on the side of the highway had not been disturbed in the slightest. Catherine stood next to the officer's car, facing the place that now lay empty of the threat she had found herself confronted with. Her eyes suddenly opened wide with shock, as she stared out into empty space. Now, her illness had come screaming out of remission, and she found herself trapped in the twisted, disconnected world of a full-blown psychosis. She turned back to the officer, desperately trying to compose herself, despite the confusion that ran rampant through her mind.

"I'm fine… really, I'm fine," she said, bringing her hands up in reassurance.

“I got into an argument with someone in town… and I just needed to vent.”

“Are you sure?” the officer cautiously asked.

“I can take you to the hospital if you want.”

“No… no, I don't need a hospital!” she said, trying to sound calm. “I'm fine, really. I'm just fine.”

Catherine took a deep breath, trying to convince the officer that she was now calm and in control.

“Well, okay…” the officer replied.

“You have a good day now.”

He was still a bit suspicious but was persuaded enough by Catherine's demeanor to drive off. After the officer drove away, Catherine looked back, searching for any sign that someone may have been there. She found nothing and the only thing she heard was the low distant howl of the warm summer wind, wandering through the valley.

# Chapter 11

Still facing the side of the road where only moments ago, Catherine was confronted with what seemed like an overwhelming evil, she slowly backed away toward her car. She moved with knees bent and in a slightly crouched position, as though prepared to fight should the men suddenly return. But, paying little attention to where her steps were taking her, she strayed near the white line that lay along the side of the highway. Catherine, still remaining with her mind frozen in terror, became startled into a scream as a passing car blared its horn. It passed close enough to her that its speeding steel bulk calls her hair to fly in its windy wake. She covered her eyes and quickly turned her back to the road as if preparing for the impact that would surely end her life. The faceless driver continued blaring their horn, even after passing her in all though still caught in a frenzy of fear, Catherine's sudden hyper-alertness detected every blast diminish in tone as the car increased its distance from her.

When all seemed quiet again, she uncovered her eyes and glanced around, as though trying to confirm any absence of the maliciousness that had previously crept into her thoughts. Catherine suddenly bolted to her car, started the engine, and quickly continued her panicked return home. She became lost in her frenzied obsession to be home, to be safe with Ivan curled up at her side. This obsession was so consuming that Catherine had become completely unaware that her speed was rapidly approaching 80 miles an hour. Easing up on the gas, she spent the next 15 minutes in absolute focus on the road ahead of her, while quietly whispering to herself about the men she saw on the road.

"They're not getting near me. I know what they want… I know what they all want. They just want to fuck me, don't you?!"
Catherine muttered to herself. "God dammit, if you fucking touch me, I'm going to kill all of you! You got that?! So stay the fuck away from me, you assholes!"

Her fear easily transformed itself into rage, and Catherine became easily consumed by it. She continued her flight of fury down the hot summer pavement, toward the security of home when, perhaps by force of habit, she glanced up into the rearview mirror. But, instead of seeing the road behind her receding into the distance, she was horrified to see a face glaring back at her from the back seat. She didn't recognize the face at a glance, but it spoke to her.

"Cat, don't you want to come back and play with us?" the voice said.

Its tone was both teasing as well as menacing, and Catherine heard it coming from directly behind her head. She stomped her foot on the brake and fishtailed the car to a stop, leaving an eighty-foot stretch of rubber down the asphalt. Catherine leaped out of her car and stared into the backseat as she slowly backed away. The car was empty, but this was not enough to convince her that what she saw was the product of her rapidly crumbling mental state. She suddenly feared, not for her sanity, but for her very life, and became completely immersed in things that her psychosis now forced upon her.

Leaving her car still running, Catherine quickly turned and ran, fearing that whoever had been in her car would be close by, watching her – waiting for the chance to do what her mind could not even invent. She continued running and, wanting to stop for a much-needed rest, retreated into the tree line to hide from her unseen tormentor. At the sound of an approaching vehicle, Catherine would dart into the woods like a nervous deer. Not knowing who was coming terrified her just as much as the voice that came from the backseat of her car. Catherine traveled the highway on foot for roughly 30 minutes when she noticed that the sky was quickly darkening. A roll of thunder wandered its way through the valley, and a narrow curtain of rain materialized in the distant southern sky. It wasn't long before she began to notice an occasional raindrop striking her head, as well as the sharp smell of the oncoming storm. Catherine quickly retreated to the tree line at the first loud crack of thunder that brought with it a brilliant bolt of lightning that seemed to split the darkened sky. She tried to remember the skills she learned from Nancy during their frequent hikes into the Bigelow Range, but the impact of her sudden relapse left her unable to organize her thoughts.

Catherine continued to walk the highway, glancing back every few minutes, looking for the shadowy figure that spoke to her from the backseat of her car. She tried to move quietly, believing that any noise might draw its attention. Within a few minutes, the storm arrived with the ferocity of an angry God, sending rain down in sheets and cutting visibility to know more than arm's length. And as steam rose from the sun-baked pavement, the wind whipped it into eddies and whirls that gave the landscape a somewhat otherworldly appearance. The cold rain soaked Catherine to the bone as she walked with her arms tightly folded against her chest, trying to fend off the chill that by this time started her teeth chattering and her body stiff.

Chapter 12

Nancy had left the campus after her last class and upon returning home checked her answering machine. It was Monday and, knowing that Catherine had gone to her psychiatrist's appointment, became concerned when she saw that there had been no messages from her. She remembered a conversation they'd had the day before, and Catherine tearfully spoke about her fear of going back to AMHI. Nancy made her promise to ask Dr. Beach if a return to inpatient care might be on the horizon. Now, she was beginning to wonder if she'd made the mistake of pressuring Catherine at a time when she may have been at her most vulnerable. Nancy also wondered if she may have received an answer from her doctor that may not be sitting well with her.

"God, I hope she's okay," she thought.

She picked up the phone and rang Catherine's number, but only got her answering machine and, remembering how far the drive was from Stratton Pond to Farmington and back, decided to give her another 30 minutes. When that time came and went, Nancy tried a number again – still with no answer. Her intuition now took over and she became gravely concerned.

"Something's wrong," she whispered to herself.

As she was about to hang up the phone, something grabbed her attention. Usually, when she returned home, the first thing she did was turn on her TV. After teaching quantum physics all day, she needed a bit of mind candy. But this had been interrupted by an emergency announcement, and Nancy watched with rapt attention. Her concerns had become greatly magnified when she saw the images of the large storm moving up the state, with the strongest of it centered on the Carrabassett Valley.

"Shit!" Nancy said aloud.

Without the least hesitation, she flew out of her apartment and jumped into her car. She knew how long it would take to get to Stratton Pond, but she also knew that Catherine was in trouble. However, she would not realize how much until she got there – until it was too late.

Chapter 13


Catherine had been walking the highway for two hours during the storm's torrential downpour. She was cold and exhausted but still confused by the whispering of gibberish that occasionally crept into her mind. She would sometimes stop and strike the sides of her head with the palms of her hands in an attempt to exorcize the voices that made her feel as though she had somehow been violated.

"Get out!" she screamed. "Leave me the fuck alone!"
When she had a bit of energy, she would quicken her step to a jog, still glancing behind her as though running from some terrifying beast bent on consuming her.

The power of the storm that seemed to swallow up the entire valley was now in full force. In Farmington, a transformer was struck by lightning, sending all of Carrabassett Valley into darkness. And when the lights lining Route 27 suddenly went black, Catherine became frozen in t her tracks, her feet fixed in place of the fear of those things that she was unable to see. Now, the landscape became a very different place, as it lay before her a silent zoo of creatures that lived only in the blackened shadows of her fractured mind.

Startled by the imposing silence, broken only by the occasional clap of thunder, Catherine once again resumed her rapid pace down the highway. She tried not to look around at the woods for fear of being confronted by something she could not overpower. The trees that lined the highway illuminated by the intermittent flash of lightning created brief, disfigured shadows among the tall stands of pine. Through Catherine's disorganized perception, the shadows took on lives of their own, moving with the wind as though peering out at her from behind the trees. Their silent stalking only compounded her already paranoid state, leading her to believe that there was now nowhere to hide. But, in the distance lay her salvation, as Catherine saw the town of Bigelow, but only by way of the headlights of a few cars that glimmered dimly through the rain.

But, the blackness of a countryside without power still blanketed the valley and continued to terrorize Catherine with its taunting silence of the unseen. She didn't realize that she was within 3 miles of Stratton Pond road, as the rain and darkness twisted not only her perception of the woods but also time. Every step felt like and startled by the occasional clap of thunder, Catherine once again resumed her rapid pace down the highway. She tried not to look around at the woods for fear of being confronted by something she could not overpower. The trees that lined the highway illuminated by the intermittent flash of lightning created brief, disfigured shadows among the tall stands of pine. Through Catherine's disorganized perception, the shadows took on lives of their own, moving with the wind as though peering out at her from behind the trees. Their silent stalking only compounded her already paranoid state, leading her to believe that there was now nowhere to hide. But, in the distance lay her salvation, as Catherine saw the town of Bigelow, but only by way of the headlights of a few cars that glimmered dimly through the rain.

But, the blackness of the countryside without power still blanketed the valley and continued to terrorize Catherine with its taunting silence of the unseen. She didn't realize that she was only within 3 miles of Stratton Pond road, as the rain and darkness twisted not only her perception of the woods, but also time, and that every step felt like an eternity.

Catherine fixed her eyes on the road directly ahead of her feet as she walked. The highway no longer lay shrouded in the rising steam of the rain's initial onslaught but was covered with the constant spattering of drops falling from an angry sky on the way to their inevitable end. At first, she had the small benefit of feeling the slight summer warmth as it glowed from the miles of highway that would lead her home. But, with the arrival of the night's rising moon that peaked out from between the clouds, Catherine felt the already firm grip of damp cold tightening its coils around her. Yet, she continued, driven not just by fear and delusion, but by desperation and a need to survive.

Her body had stopped shivering, leaving her with a staggering gait resembling that of the walking dead. The valley remained unlit and gave Catherine the overwhelming feeling of being truly isolated and somewhat lost. But, she quickly made her way to the entrance of Stratton Pond road, in spite of the cold stiffness that clenched down on every muscle of her body. Once there, she could make out the faint image of her cabin as though it had been placed there by God, acting as a beacon in the night.

# Chapter 14

Two hours after leaving her apartment, Nancy found herself on the southern end of Route 27. She had driven into the storm about 45 minutes ago, but the rain did not slow her down, and Nancy continued driving at around 65 miles an hour. She held the wheel with an iron grip, focusing on the road ahead as though she were staring down a wild animal. Thirty minutes later, she saw flashing red and blue lights in the distance that forced a horrifying image into her mind. It displayed itself to her consciousness as if she were sitting front and center in a movie theater. She saw Catherine's car lying off the side of the highway, trailed by a long black skid mark. The front of the car was crumpled against a large pine tree midway up the windshield, which had been shattered upon impact. Some fifteen feet into the woods lay a yellow vinyl tarp that had been partially pulled back, while several police officers aimed their flashlights at a scene that would stay with them forever. Nancy's mind flashed from one disturbing image to the next like a series of photographic stills, and she now saw beneath the tarp. As the images revealed themselves to her, Catherine's body lay on the rain-soaked earth, twisted into a misshapen tangle of broken limbs. Her entire face was badly scraped after impacting against the pine tree's thick, unforgiving bark. Her nose rested against her cheek after being partially torn away by its collision with the pine tree's unmoving bulk, while the ground beneath her head soaked up the blood that had streamed from the middle of her face.

Nancy began crying as she pulled her attention from the horrific images in her mind and back to the highway. Within a few minutes, she found herself slowing down as she approached the roadblock that had been set up in front of Catherine's car. She stopped her car and, after pulling the emergency brake, jumped out and was stopped by a police officer.

"I'm sorry, Miss," he began. "But this part of the highway's been blocked off."

"But I know whose car that is!" Nancy replied with a great deal of urgency.

The officer looked at her with a slightly stunned expression, then motioned her over to the car.

"Come on over here," he said. "Maybe you can answer some questions for us." The officer led Nancy over to the car, and she immediately noticed that it was completely undamaged.

"It was found that passing motorists were just sitting here, still idling with the headlights on," the officer said.

"In this weather, it's a wonder no one hit it. Someone could've been killed."

Nancy bent down to look into the still-open driver's door while the officer aimed his flashlight into the car.

"We turned it off, trying not to disturb anything inside," the officer said as Nancy scanned the inside of the vehicle.

"You want to tell us about this?"

"Are there any footprints leading into the woods?" Nancy asked.

"No," the officer replied. "Is there something we should know about this person?" Nancy stood up and turned to the officer with a bit of hesitation.

"Well, it's a long story," she said.
They stood next to the car as the rain continued to fall while Nancy explained Catherine's condition to the officer, who wrote down as much as he could in his notepad.

"And what did you say that was called again?" the officer asked. "Schizo, what?"

"Schizophrenia," Nancy replied. "She has paranoid schizophrenia."

"Do you think she could be dangerous or become violent?" asked the officer.

"Really, I don't know," she replied.
The officer continued writing in his notepad and had he looked up into Nancy's face, he would have known that she was lying. She didn't want Catherine to be treated like a common criminal or some kind of escaped lunatic, and if the police

had the chance to approach her, she wanted to be there as a calming, familiar face. "Are you sure there aren't any tracks going into the woods?" Nancy asked.

"We didn't find any," the officer replied. "But the storm probably washed away any tracks that may have been in the area."

"What about a search party?" Nancy asked. The officer shook his head.

"Not in this weather," he said. "It'd be impossible to find anything in these woods right now, especially at night, and we can't take the chance of risking other people for only one person."

Nancy knew that the officer was right, but she couldn't help feeling somewhat appalled by the idea of simply giving up on another human being, regardless of the circumstances.

"Look, I'm sorry about your friend," the officer said. "But, if it makes you feel any better, we did call in a helicopter to search the surrounding woods. It's not likely that they're going to see anything through all of this dense cover, but there may be a few small clearings they can search."

Just as the officer finished his words, he heard the distant buzz of an approaching helicopter, and within moments it was roaring over their heads. Its blades slashed through the night air while a large searchlight pierced the dark sky like a hot wire through butter.

"Do you have any idea where she may have gone?" the officer asked.

The sound of the helicopter beating its blades against the cold air forced the officer to yell to be heard.

"Catherine would have gone someplace where she felt safe!" Nancy replied.
She had also found herself yelling as the helicopters circled for another pass.

"How long are you going to keep looking?"

"It's hard to say," the officer replied. "There's a second front coming in."

"You can't just leave her out there!" Nancy protested.

"I wish the weather was more cooperative," he said. "But we're doing everything we can."

Nancy nodded her head and returned to her car. She sat in the front seat with her forehead resting on the wheel and her hands on the sides of her head. Trying to maintain some semblance of clarity, she was suddenly struck with what the officers had missed.

"Someplace safe," she whispered to herself. She realized now that the police were so busy looking for Catherine that they had overlooked the obvious. Nancy started her car, backed up about ten feet, drove around the roadblock along the left side of the highway, and headed north. She had a strong feeling that Catherine may have tried to make her way home. Even in this weather, she may be driven enough by fear and paranoia to try to get home on foot. Nancy turned her high beams on and, as she drove up Route 27, began searching the sides of the road. The Carrabassett Valley was known not only for its beauty. But its dense pine forests and not a summer went by without a few hikers getting lost. And it was always expected that some of them would never be found.

# Chapter 15

Catherine staggered up to the door of her cabin, exhausted and soaked by the cold rain. She tried the doorknob and somehow, through the haze of psychotic confusion, she realized that she left her keys in her car. Catherine knew that she was physically unable to return to her car, and peering through the window her weakened body against the door. Unable to budge it even slightly, she turned her back to the door and slid down to a sitting position on the cold, wet ground. With her elbows on her knees, she cradled her forehead with her hands and began crying, desperate for a way out of the nightmare she was living. Her tears suddenly turned to anger as she rose to her feet and screamed, punching a jagged hole in one of the four panes of the front door. Just as quickly, she pulled her fist out from the glassy irregular hole, but shock and her state of mind would not allow Catherine to feel the gashes that the glass had carved down her arm and hand. She opened the door from the inside and, darting into her cabin, quickly slammed it shut, as if to keep someone or something from forcing its way in. She found her way to a light switch, completely unaware that the wounds on her hand and arm now pattered blood that followed her in a trail across the floor. Forgetting that the entire valley had been cast into darkness, Catherine hit the light switch, and when nothing happened she suddenly felt lost in her own home.

"Fuck, what now?!" she said.

Then she remembered Ivan, who made it a habit of hiding under her bed during thunderstorms. She crawled along the floor, making her way to her bedroom, and peering under the bed, saw Ivan as a quivering bundle of nervous fur.

"Ivan," she said, with a gentle voice.

"Come here, baby. Mommy's here."

Ivan looked up and chirped gently, but when Catherine reached back for him, he reared back and hissed loudly. She gasped and reflexively pulled her hand back as he growled at her slightly, his eyes turning red like glowing embers in the night. Her breathing became panicked as Catherine backed out of her bedroom and slammed the door shut. Without Ivan there to comfort her, she became fully aware of how alone she was but, she still couldn't find her way through the house.

Out across the treetops, a pulse of lightning lit the sky in warning of the destructive force still to come. Somehow, through the chaotic torment that ran rampant through her mind, she experienced a brief moment of clarity and saw an opportunity. Whenever the lightning illuminated the inside of the house, Catherine would use it to gain her bearings and to see where she needed to go. She had stored candles and knew exactly where they were. It was now just a matter of getting to them. Catherine made her way to a small closet just off the kitchen and frantically felt around the shelves. She soon laid her hands on the candles, as well as a candleholder and a box of stick matches. Lighting one of the matches, she was now able to see well enough to put a candle in the brass holder and as the wick burned, the inside of the house took on an eerie glow.

Still shivering from the cold, Catherine went to the couch and, grabbing the throw that covered it, threw it around her shoulders. She heard the rain intensify again and went over to her phone to call Nancy. She desperately needed to talk to her, but the line was dead. Cursing to herself, she hung up the phone and turned back toward the kitchen when a brilliant bolt of lightning tore its way across the sky. Its white flash revealed the dark silhouette of a large-framed stranger peering at her through her kitchen window. Catherine screamed in terror as the faceless stranger placed a hand up on the window pane.
"Go away!" she screamed.
She backed up toward the couch and, covering her eyes, began to hyperventilate again. When she looked back up at the window, the large dark figure had disappeared.

She ran to the medicine cabinet in the bathroom and holding the candle up she opened its mirrored door. It was only now that she saw her hand, lacerated by the jagged glass of the window she was forced to break to get into her cabin. But, she still felt no pain, due mostly to exhaustion and shock. Catherine rummaged through the cabinet, looking for the one thing she believed would take away the demons that haunted her mind.

"Where the fuck is it?!" she screamed. Within moments, she had pushed the contents of the medicine cabinet out onto the floor and was now on her hands and knees in a panicked search.

"Shit!" Catherine cursed, with both desperation and frustration.

She set the candle on the floor and used both hands to examine every box, jar, and bottle until finding a prescription bottle of Lorazepam. Catherine's violently trembling hands opened the bottle, spilling its contents across the floor. As she hurriedly reached for the round white pills, her fumbling hands knocked over the candle.

Once again, in complete darkness, she clutched one of the pills in her fist and crawled over to a corner of the bathroom. She curled up in the fetal position while frantically putting the pill under her tongue. It wasn't more than a few minutes until it had completely melted and entered her bloodstream, but it would take time for it to take effect. Catherine again became concerned about Ivan as she heard him crying and scratching against the bedroom door. She was still in a state of terror, but Ivan's cries caused her maternal instincts to suddenly overwhelm her fears, as well as her sense of caution. Catherine crowned out of the bathroom and through the contents of the medicine cabinet that lay strewn across the floor.

"Ivan?" she called. "Mommy's coming."
 She paused briefly to wipe the tears from her eyes, then continued across the floor, stopping at the bedroom door. With the next flash of lightning, she saw one of Ivan's paws exploring the space between the door and the hardwood floor. Catherine reached up and turning the doorknob cracked the door open by an inch or two.

"Mommy's right here," she said.
Her voice was gentle and calming, but still quivering with fear and confusion. Ivan pressed his face against the space created by the slightly open door and began licking her fingers as she touched his nose in an attempt to comfort him.

"Mommy will let you out as soon as she has the lights back on, okay?"
She carefully closed the door, confining Ivan to the bedroom again, and, rising to her feet, turned to cautiously make her way through the darkness and back into the living room. Catherine felt her way back to the closet for another candle, and this time she found them with a great deal less effort. She also found a wooden candleholder as well as

some stick matches. Catherine knew that somewhere in the house was a flashlight, but in her psychotic haze she was unable to remember where it was.

Again, she lit a candle and was able to see well enough to push it down into the candleholder. Catherine stood up and, after turning back toward the living room, suddenly screamed as a familiar figure stood before her.

"Daddy?" she said.

Her voice was panicked, and again she began hyperventilating as the sight of her dead father pushed her back against the wall.

"No…no. But you're…"

She tried to shake the image from her mind and, looking back up, found that the figure of her father remained unmoved with unblinking eyes fixed upon her. Standing in the walkway of her living room, he stood dressed in the suit he'd been buried in, covered with smears of dirt and stains of decay. His face was pale and as his eyes stood open in a wide gaze, a plastic eye cap, previously inserted by a funeral technician, dislodged itself with an almost silent pop and slid down his cheek, landing on the floor. Catherine covered her mouth and gagged slightly as she witnessed this grotesque scene when the figure spoke. Cocking his head slightly to one side as a thin trail of green tinged fluid ran out of his nose and slowly down his cheek.

"Cat," he said.

It was indeed her father's voice, but devoid of personality or life, forcing Catherine's eyes back up to his face.

"This isn't happening…this isn't happening," she repeated to herself.

"You're dead! I saw you die!"

"Cat," he repeated.  "None of this is real."

"No!" Catherine screamed.

Nothing made sense to her anymore, and turning away from the pale figure, she ran a few steps to the kitchen and grabbed a cast iron pan. She ran the three or four steps back to the living room, but in her haste dropped the candle and was once again in the dark. However, the darkness didn't stop her from swinging the pan through the air.

"You're dead!" she screamed.

Her voice was filled with rage as she searched through the darkened living room for something she could no longer see.

"Where the fuck are you?!" she yelled.

There was no response, and she continued to swing the heavy cast iron pan at the empty air.


Catherine stopped in the middle of her battle with the imaginary corpse when a pair of lights appeared in front of her cabin. After going out, there was a brief silence, then a tapping on the front door. Nancy had finally arrived after leaving the roadblock where Catherine's car remained on the highway.

"Cath?" Nancy called. "It's me, Nancy, are you alright?"

 She discovered the small pane of glass that had been broken and noticed blood on the doorknob. She quickly came to the conclusion that Catherine was inside and considering the conditions she walked through to get home, Nancy felt that Catherine would be in dire need of medical attention.

Upon hearing Nancy knock at the front door, Catherine crouched down around the corner from the living room just inside the entrance to the kitchen. She still clutched the cast iron pan tightly in her hands and began whispering gibberish to herself. Opening the door by only a few inches, Nancy looked cautiously around the living room. She always carried a small pen light for safety, and taking it out of her pocket cast its dim light around the house. Seeing nothing but furniture and bits of broken glass, Nancy slowly stepped into the cabin. She heard the crunch of glass underfoot, and she took a first step through the doorway. As she took another step, she again called out to Catherine.

"Cath, it's Nancy. Everything's going to be okay."

She wanted Catherine to feel comforted by the sound of her voice, but Catherine was still fighting the demons that forced their way into her mind – violating her every thought.

Nancy continued walking slowly through the house, making her way around the end of the couch. Shining her penlight on the floor, she stopped when the light fell on the candle that now lay broken in half and dislodged from the candleholder. The lightning still flashed outside, creating eerie shadows among the furniture and trinkets that had been carefully organized in the living room. Now, she was certain that Catherine was in the house and thought that she was likely in her bedroom, trying to hide from the storm. However, as she approached the corner that turned off toward the kitchen, Catherine suddenly appeared in the dull beam of Nancy's penlight. Her clothes were still soaked from the rain and her hair had become matted down to her head. Catherine glared at her with an angry, wild look and began screaming as she swung the heavy pan, striking Nancy against the side of her head near her left eye.

"Don't touch me!" Catherine screamed. Nancy was forced back a step by the impact, dropping her penlight and staggering slightly as her hand went to the place that now felt as though it was on fire.

"Cath, it's me, Nancy!" she pleaded. She raised her other hand, holding it out, trying to fend off any continued attacks, but Catherine stepped toward her and swung from the other direction. This time, the pan landed solidly against

Nancy's forearm, breaking both bones and leaving it in an obvious state of disfigurement. Nancy screamed from the sudden onset of fiery pain and dropped to her knees.

"Cath, listen to me!" she begged tearfully. "It's Nancy! I just…"
Her words were cut short by another blow to the side of her head, and it was with that Nancy lost consciousness, landing hard on the living room floor.
Catherine's exhaustion had now been replaced by a state of psychotic rage, as she continued to scream with each swing of the cast iron pan.

"Get the fuck out!" she screamed. "I saw you die!"
She swung the pan repeatedly from side to side, throwing heavy trails of blood across the walls and up onto the ceiling. By the time Catherine had become physically exhausted, Nancy's head and face had taken on the appearance of a bloody, half rotten jack o' lantern. Her jaw had become grossly dislocated and several bones in her skull and face were fractured. Nancy had been severely beaten beyond all hope and as she exhaled her last breath, Catherine stepped back, dropping the pan to the floor where it landed with a loud thud.

Catherine stared at Nancy's lifeless body and through an almost imperceptibly brief window of lucidity, now realized that she'd bludgeoned her best friend to death. She screamed and dropped to her knees, where she began crying hysterically. All Catherine wanted to do now was run away – away from her haunted mind; away from the reality that lay sprawled out on her living room floor. She got back to her feet and continued stepping away from the gruesome scene that had played out by her own hand.

"I'm sorry… Nancy, I'm sorry," she said, with a whimper in her voice.

"I didn't mean to… I swear."

Unable to absorb the reality of killing her closest friend, Catherine became caught in a moment of blind panic. She ran to the front door and, throwing it open with enough force to shatter another of its windows, left the cabin in ran blindly down Stratton Brook Road towards the highway. She didn't know where she was running, she just wanted to get away and upon reaching the end of the road, Catherine crossed the first lane of Route 27. As she entered the middle of the next lane, she was frozen in place by the lights of an oncoming car. Her eyes widened with terror as, for a brief instant, she saw the driver's expression – the look of panic and anticipated horror; the moment when time freezes to an icy halt. She felt a momentary impact and seemed to float away as the car's tires ground to a stop on the wet asphalt. Catherine landed hard on the pavement with the back of her head striking the roadway, immediately rendering her unconscious and splitting her scalp into a bloody gaping wound. As the hands of time once again commenced their motion, Catherine's skidding body came to a stop.

The driver leaped from his car and ran to her side, not wanting to move her for fear of worsening her injuries. He got down on his knees and leaning over called to her.

"Miss, Hey! Wake up!" he yelled.
But Catherine showed no signs of waking, and from where she lay there was nothing – no numbness, no stars of twilight consciousness fading from a field of blackened sight. From the back of her head, blood streamed across the pavement like a river at its crest and her pupils became dim, growing to the size of no return. As her body lay on the highway, her soul took flight like a startled bird as another flicker of lightning cast its reflection off of her open, lifeless eyes.

# Chapter 16

The stranger left his cell phone on, staying in touch with the 911 operator while attempting CPR on Catherine's body. A few minutes later, the police arrived, having suspected that the abandoned car on Route 27 was connected to the woman that lay on the wet pavement. With an ambulance in tow, the area was surrounded, and the highway blocked off in both directions. The paramedics pronounced Catherine dead at the scene and as her body was zipped into a long gray bag, the streetlights at the intersection flickered back to life. And after the police had spread out over the area, an officer noticed some footprints in the mud just inside the entrance of Stratton Brook Road. He followed the tracks down the rain-soaked road and spotted the cabin, with a single light from the living room shining out into the wooded darkness. Approaching the cabin, he noticed the car parked in front, as well as the wide open front door and glass shards that lay strewn about the doorway. Leaning his head in through the doorway, he also discovered Nancy's body sprawled out in the living room, the side of her face sticking to the floor as she lay in a large pool of blood.

The officer radioed back, reporting that he'd found a second body in a cabin at the end of

Stratton Brook Road. It didn't take long for other officers to converge on the small house and after Catherine's body had been loaded into the ambulance, the paramedics soon followed. Nancy was also pronounced dead, but because she appeared to die as the result of violence, the police were forced to investigate it as a homicide. After the police photographed her body, Nancy was rolled over by the paramedics and prepared for transport. Upon turning her body over, the side of her face became unglued from the pool of blood that had cemented it to the floor. The separation of skin from hardwood made a wet, peeling sound that sent one officer racing for the door, while others forced their tongues against the roofs of their mouths, trying to fight off the same reaction.

The police continued to photograph the living room as well as the kitchen where the cast iron pan landed, leaving a noticeable dent in the floor. They photographed the living room floor, where Nancy's body lay only minutes ago, as well as the walls and ceiling that had been spattered with blood. But as the pan was being put into an evidence bag and the blood spots were being swabbed, Catherine's phone rang. Every officer stopped what they were doing and stared at it as the answering machine switched on. The lead detective ordered that no one was to touch the phone or the answering machine. What they heard next brought tears to the eyes of every officer within earshot.

"Hi Catherine, it's mom. We lost power because of the storm, but everything's back on now. Give me a call when you get a chance, and remember to take your meds. Talk to you later. Love you."

Outside the occasional car accident, nothing like this had ever happened in Carrabassett Valley, and the peaceful tranquility of the valley's natural beauty was now permanently scarred. One or two of the officers at the scene would eventually resign, having been pushed over the limits of their emotional insulation. But, the events that unfolded in that small cabin, nestled in the idyllic woods of Maine's Bigelow Mountains, changed the lives of everyone and would forever leave a cloud of tragedy over the people of the Carrabassett Valley.

End

www.ingramcontent.com/pod-product-compliance
Lightning Source LLC
Chambersburg PA
CBHW061517050726
47593CB00002B/613